The Mystery of The Strange Bundle

The Tenth Adventure of
the Five Find-Outers and
Buster the Dog

Granada Publishing Limited
Published in 1969 by Dragon Books
Frogmore, St Albans, Herts AL2 2NF
Reprinted 1970, 1971 (twice), 1972, 1973, 1974, 1975, 1976

First published by Methuen & Co Ltd 1952
Copyright © Enid Blyton 1952

Made and printed in Great Britain by
C. Nicholls & Company Ltd
The Philips Park Press, Manchester
Set in Intertype Times

The Mystery of
The Strange Bundle

Enid Blyton

Cover illustration by Mary Gernat
Text illustrations by Jenny Chapple

Dragon

The Five Find-Outers met in Fatty's shed

"Of all the miserable holidays these just about beat the lot!" said Pip to Bets. "Why you had to start us off on this awful 'flu' I can't imagine!"

Bets looked hurt. "Well, I couldn't help it," she said. "Someone gave it to me before I gave it to you others. It was jolly bad luck that it happened at Christmas."

Pip blew his nose violently. He was sitting up in bed, feeling decidedly better but very bad-tempered.

"*You* get it as soon as the Christmas hols begin – and you get it lighter than any one! Then you give it to Daisy, and she gives it to Larry, and they have it all through Christmas, poor things. And then *I* get it, and poor old Fatty. What a mess-up of the Christmas hols! Hardly any left of them now!"

Pip sounded very cross indeed. Bets got up. "All right. If you're going to be such a crosspatch I won't sit with you this morning. I'll go and see Fatty. I think you're very unkind, Pip, after all the games I've played with you and the books I've read you."

She was just stalking out with her head in the air, looking very high and mighty, when Pip called to her.

"Hey, Bets – tell Fatty I'm feeling better, and ask him to get on the track of some mystery AT ONCE, because I feel it's just the kind of tonic I need. And we've only got about ten days of the hols left."

Bets grinned round at him. "All right. I'll tell him. But Fatty can't just spin a mystery out of thin air, Pip. I think we'll have to go without one this hols."

"Fatty can do *anything*," said Pip, with the utmost conviction. "I've been lying here for days, and most of the time I've been remembering all the mysteries we've ever solved with old Fatty. I've never had time to do so much thinking before. Old Fatty's a wonder."

"I knew that without having to do a lot of thinking," said Bets. "All his disguises – and the way he works out

5

the clues – and the tricks he's played on Mr. Goon."

"Oh yes!" said Pip, a broad smile on his pale face. "I say – it makes me feel better even to think of all those fat-headed tricks of Fatty's. For goodness' sake tell Fatty to work up some mystery or other for us – it'll do us all good. Give us some interest in life!"

"I'm going," said Bets. "I'll bring a mystery back for you if I can!"

"Bring some peppermints too," said Pip. "I've suddenly got a craving for them. No, bring a bagful of bull's-eyes, the hottest you can buy. I could do with about fifty, Bets, to go with this detective book Fatty's lent me."

"You *must* be feeling better!" said Bets. She went out of the room and put on her outdoor things. She took some money out of her money-box. She meant to buy Fatty something too. Bets had been a very faithful visitor and friend to the rest of the Find-Outers while they had had the "flu" and had spent nearly all her Christmas money on them.

She hadn't been able to help feeling guilty about giving everyone the "flu" and she had tried to make up for it by playing games with the invalids, reading to them, and taking them anything she thought they would like. Fatty had been very touched with the little girl's kindness. He thought the world of Bets.

Bets looked out of the garden door. Should she take her bicycle or not? It was so much quicker on a bike. She decided against it. The roads were slippery that frosty January day.

She walked down to the village and spent a good deal of money on enormous bull's-eye peppermints. Half for Pip and half for Fatty. If Pip had got to the convalescent stage of craving for sweets then presumably Fatty would soon reach it too!

She came out of the shop in time to see Mr. Goon, the village policeman, sail slowly down the road on his bicycle, his nose purple with the cold air of the morning.

He saw Bets and put on his brakes too quickly. His bicycle immediately skidded on the slippery surface and

Mr. Goon found himself sitting down very suddenly in the middle of the road.

"Gah!" he said, glaring at Bets as if it was her fault.

"Oh, Mr. Goon – are you hurt?" cried Bets. "You sat down with such a bump!"

Mr. Goon had plenty to sit down on, so he wasn't hurt, only considerably shaken. He got up and brushed down his trousers.

"These here slippery mornings'll be the death of me," he said, looking at Bets as if she were responsible for the slipperiness. "I just put my brakes on, see – and down I came! That's all I get for wanting to be polite and to ask after your friends. I did hear they were all down with this here 'flu'."

"Yes – but they're getting better," said Bets.

Mr. Goon muttered something that sounded like "What a pity!" He straddled his bicycle again. "Well, I must say it's been a real change for me not having that nosey-parker of a fat boy sticking his nose into *my* business all the time he's home for the holidays," said Mr. Goon. "It's a funny thing how that boy sniffs out anything that's going, and gets you all into it. A good thing he's had to lie up in bed where he's out of mischief. You'll be back at school again in no time – and for once in a way you won't have made nuisances of yourselves."

"You'll get the 'flu' yourself if you talk like that," said Bets, stung into boldness. She was usually very scared of the policeman, especially if she met him when she was alone. "Anyway, there's still time for something to crop up – and if it does, we'll be on the job long before *you* are, Mr. Goon!"

And, feeling rather victorious after this unexpected meeting and exchange of talk, Bets marched off with her head in the air.

"If you're seeing that fat boy, tell him it's nice to know he's been kept out of mischief for once in a way!" Mr. Goon shouted after her. "I've been having a nice peaceful time, I have, without you five round my feet all the time – to say nothing of that little pest of a dog!"

7

Bets pretended not to hear. Mr. Goon pedalled off, well satisfied. He guessed Bets would repeat everything and he knew Fatty would be mad with him – but before he could make himself a nuisance he'd be back at school again. Toad of a boy!

Bets went to Fatty's house, let herself in at the garden door, and found Mrs. Trotteville, Fatty's mother. Mrs. Trotteville was fond of the little girl and smiled at her.

"Well, Bets – come to see Frederick again? You really are a faithful friend. I think he must be feeling distinctly better today. I've heard the most peculiar noises coming from his room whenever I go up on the landing!"

"Oh – you don't think he's been sick again, do you?" said Bets, in alarm. "What sort of noises?"

"Oh, voices and sounds," said Mrs. Trotteville. "As if he's rehearsing for a play or something. You know what Frederick is – always up to something."

Bets nodded. She thought probably Fatty was practising various voices for his different disguises. An old man's voice – a quavering old woman's – a deep, manly voice. Fatty could imitate them all to perfection!

"I'll take you up to his room," said Mrs. Trotteville. "He's expecting you."

They went upstairs. Mrs. Trotteville gave a sharp knock at Fatty's door.

"Who is it?" said Fatty's voice. "I've got a visitor, Mother!"

Mrs. Trotteville looked astonished. As far as she knew no other visitor had arrived that morning. It must have been some one the cook had ushered upstairs. She turned the handle and she and Bets went into the room.

Fatty appeared to be sunk deeply into his pillows, half asleep. Bets could see his dark, rumpled hair but that was about all. Her heart sank. Yesterday Fatty had been sitting up, looking quite sprightly. He couldn't be feeling so well if he felt more like lying down!

She looked at his visitor. It was a plump, bespectacled woman, with an ugly, pudding-shaped black hat pulled over her forehead. A bright green scarf was wound round her neck, hiding part of her chin. Who on earth was she?

Mrs. Trotteville was at a loss too. Who was this strange visitor? She advanced towards her uncertainly.

"Oh – Mrs. Trotteville!" said the visitor, in a mincing kind of voice. "You don't remember me, do you? We met at Bollingham two years ago. *Such* a nice place, wasn't it?"

"Er no – I don't think I *do* remember you," said Mrs. Trotteville, astonished. "How did you know Frederick was ill – and who brought you up to his room? Really, er – it's kind of you – but . . ."

"Oh, your nice cook brought me up," chattered the visitor, mopping her face with a large white handkerchief drenched with some strong scent. "She said you were busy so she just brought me up herself. Frederick was *so* pleased to see me. And who is this nice little girl?"

Bets was puzzled. She didn't understand this curious visitor. And why didn't Fatty sit up? Why hadn't he spoken to Bets? She looked at the mound his body made under the clothes. He must be asleep!

She poked him hard. "Fatty! Wake up! You were awake a minute ago, because you spoke to us when we knocked at the door. Sit up and speak to me!"

Fatty took no notice. He just lay there like a log. Mrs. Trotteville began to feel alarmed. She, too, went to the bed and touched Fatty.

"Frederick – are you all right? Sit up, do!"

Bets glanced at the visitor, who had now got up and was looking out of the window, her back to them. Her shoulders were shaking slightly. What WAS the matter? It was very peculiar and mysterious and Bets didn't like it at all.

Mrs. Trotteville turned back the covers of the bed. There was no Fatty there! A dark wig had been put over a pudding-basin, and bolsters had been laid in the bed. Mrs. Trotteville gave a little scream.

"Fatty! Where's Fatty!"

But Bets knew where he was, of course!

Bets swung round on the plump woman standing at the window. She ran to her and grabbed her arm. She shook it hard.

"Fatty! Fatty, you terror! You're your own visitor. Oh, *Fatty*!"

The "visitor" collapsed into a chair. Loud explosions came from her. Yes – it was certainly Fatty all right. There was no mistaking that explosive laughter!

"*Frederick!*" said his mother, amazed and annoyed. "Are you out of your mind? You're supposed to be in bed. What in the world are you thinking of, getting up and dressing in this ridiculous way? No, it's not funny. I'm vexed. I shall tell the doctor when he comes. Get those clothes off and get back into bed at once."

"Oh, Mother, give me a minute to laugh," gasped Fatty, still collapsed in the chair. "It was too comic to see you and Bets poking at me to make me speak, and wondering who the visitor was, and trying to be polite to her." And Fatty went off into great laughs again.

"Well, all I can say is that you must be feeling a lot better if you can get up to such silly antics," said Mrs. Trotteville, still annoyed. "I suppose such abnormal behaviour must mean that your temperature is normal again. Frederick, get back into bed again at once. No – not with those awful clothes on – where *did* you get them from?"

"Cookie brought them for me from an old aunt of hers," said Fatty, pulling off the bright green scarf and the awful old hat. "They're part of my wardrobe of disguises, Mother. Don't pretend you don't know!"

Mrs. Trotteville often had to turn a blind eye on many of Fatty's doings. There was simply no knowing what he would get up to next. She stared at the clothes in disgust.

"Dirty old things!" she said. "And that *awful* scent, Frederick. I really can't even *call* it perfume! I shall have to open the window and let out the smell."

"Yes, do," said Fatty. "I can't bear much more of it myself. Gosh, I did enjoy that. Here, Bets, hang up this long black coat and skirt in my big wardrobe over there."

He stripped off coat and skirt, and appeared in his striped pyjamas. Bets didn't think that the "flu" had made him lose weight at all. She took the coat and skirt, and was about to hang them up when Mrs. Trotteville took them away from her.

"No. They must go to be cleaned if Frederick *must* keep them," she said. "I really must tell Cook not to unload her aunt's old clothes on to him."

"Mother, don't you dare to say a word," said Fatty, in alarm. "Cook's a marvel. She lets me have her uncle's old things too. I've got to get proper disguises from *some*-where. You know perfectly well I'm going to be a first-class detective as soon as I'm old enough, and you have to begin practising young. Don't you say a word to Cook!"

"Frederick, I am *not* going to have the house full of the smelly old garments belonging to Cook's uncle and aunt," said his mother firmly.

"You needn't," almost wailed Fatty. "I usually keep them down in my shed at the bottom of the garden – don't I, Bets? I just wanted to play this visitor trick on Bets, Mother, that's all – so I got Cook to fetch these things from the shed for me. Bets can take them down to the shed this very minute if you want her to."

Fatty was now in bed. He looked beseechingly at Bets and his mother. Mrs. Trotteville thought that he had suddenly gone rather pale. All this silly excitement!

"All right, Frederick. We won't say any more," she said. "Bets can take the things down when she goes. Put them out on the landing for now, Bets. Frederick, lie down. I'm sure your temperature must be going up again. I certainly shan't let you get up for a short while this afternoon if so."

"Mother, can Bets stay and have lunch with me," said Fatty, changing the subject quickly. He fully intended to get up that afternoon! "Say she can. None of the

11

others is coming to see me today, they're still wobbly. I'd like Bets' company – and you know she's quiet. She'd be very good for me. Wouldn't you, Bets?"

Bets beamed. To spend the day with Fatty would be marvellous. Pip was in the bad-tempered stage and too difficult to get on with amiably at the moment. It would be wizard to stay with Fatty! She gazed hopefully at Mrs. Trotteville, her arms full of the smelly old clothes.

Mrs. Trotteville considered. "Well, yes, I think if Bets would like to stay she would probably keep you from doing any further ridiculous things," she said. "Would you like to stay, Bets dear? And promise me that you won't let Fatty leap out of bed, or dress up, or play the fool in any way at all?"

"I promise," said Bets happily. "Thank you, Mrs. Trotteville."

"I'll telephone to your mother and see if it's all right," said Mrs. Trotteville, and disappeared out of the room. Bets beamed again, and Fatty beamed back.

"Good old Bets," said Fatty, snuggling down in bed. "Gosh. I nearly burst when you and Mother kept poking at the bolster in the bed. It wasn't a very good disguise really, but it was the best I could do on the spur of the moment. I feel better today and I was longing for a joke of some kind. I guessed you'd be coming, so I got Cookie to fetch me those things from the shed. She's a pet, is Cookie."

"You must have been annoyed when your mother came in too!" said Bets. "Oh, Fatty – it's nice that you're better. Have a peppermint? They're the biggest bull's-eyes I could buy. There's half for you and half for Pip."

"I must be a lot better," said Fatty, taking two peppermints and putting them both in his mouth at once. "I couldn't possibly have even *sniffed* at a bull's-eye yesterday. I shouldn't be a bit surprised if I eat a lot of dinner today."

"You look awfully pale, Fatty," said Bets. "Lie down for a bit. You really shouldn't have got out of bed and dressed up like that."

"Now don't you start lecturing!" said Fatty. "My legs do feel a bit funny, actually, but it was worth it. Now – spill the news. Have you got any?"

Bets faithfully gave her news. Fatty lay quiet and listened. He was feeling rather faint, but he wasn't going to tell Bets that! He hadn't realized that the effort of getting up and dressing and playing the fool would make him feel so queer. Apparently you couldn't play about with "flu" too much even if you *were* feeling better!

"Larry and Daisy are much better," said Bets. "They're both up and about now, though they haven't been out yet. Daisy says they'll be out tomorrow if it's sunny. They're most frightfully bored, though, and keep wishing something would happen."

"How's Pip?" asked Fatty.

"Oh, he's better, except in his temper," said Bets. "Don't you go and get bad-tempered too, Fatty, when you're almost better! Oh – and I nearly forgot to tell you – I met Mr. Goon this morning!"

"Ah – the great Goon," said Fatty, half-sitting up at the mention of his old enemy's name. "And what had *he* to say?"

"Well, he said 'Gah' at me, fell off his bicycle, and sat down hard in the road," said Bets, with a giggle.

"Couldn't be better," said Fatty, hard-heartedly. "And what else had he got to say beside 'Gah'?"

Bets told him. "He said he'd had a nice peaceful time without that nosey-parker of a fat boy interfering all the time," she said. "He was really rather rude. He said it was a good thing you were in bed and out of mischief – and you'd be back at school again before you'd time to *do* any!"

"Ha!" said Fatty, sitting up straight now, and looking very determined. "That's what he thinks, does he? Well, I'll be up proper tomorrow – and out the next day – and Goon had better be on his guard. Things will happen as soon as I'm up!"

"What things?" asked Bets, thrilled. "A mystery, do you mean? Oh, Fatty!"

"Yes – a Mystery – even if I have to make one up

13

myself," said Fatty. "If Goon thinks he's *ever* going to have a nice peaceful holiday when we're home, he's wrong. Bets, we'll have some fun when I'm up. Gosh, it makes me feel better again already to think of it."

"What sort of fun?" asked Bets, her eyes shining. "Oh, Fatty, I wish a real mystery would turn up again – but there isn't time now – we'll all be back at school before we could solve it – if one *did* turn up!"

"Never mind – we'll have some fun with old Goon first," said Fatty. "I'll plan it. We'll all be in it. I'll think up something, don't you worry."

Bets knew he would. There was absolutely no one like Fatty for thinking up things. He slithered down into bed again and shut his eyes.

"Are you feeling all right?" asked Bets anxiously.

"Gosh, yes – I just got an idea, that's all," said Fatty. "You know how ideas come – all in a flash from your imagination – you don't even have to think of them."

"They don't come to *me* like that," said Bets. "I have to think hard before I dig up an idea – and even then it's hardly ever a good one. You're a genius, Fatty!"

"Well," said Fatty, modestly, "I wouldn't quite say *that*, you know – but I can make rings round most people, can't I? I mean – look how we've solved all those mysteries when I've been on the job, and . . ."

Fatty spent the next ten minutes unashamedly boasting, and Bets listened, unashamedly worshipping the boaster. In fact, they both had a very nice time.

"What's the time?" said Fatty suddenly. "Surely it *must* be dinner-time, Bets. Have you got any more bull's-eyes for me? I'm starving."

"I think I can hear dinner coming now," said Bets. "Yes – it's your mother. I'll go and help her with the trays."

Mrs. Trotteville appeared, bearing a tray with two steaming platefuls of soup. Fatty eyed them in disappointment. "Oh, Mother! Soup again! When am I going to have a real decent meal? I'll never get better on soup!"

"You said yesterday that you couldn't possibly take

14

even a spoonful of soup!" said his mother, putting the tray down. "Don't worry. There's roast chicken and all the etceteras if you want some."

"That's better," said Fatty. "What's the pudding? Save me two holpings, Mother."

Mrs. Trotteville laughed. "Oh, Frederick – you do go to extremes. All right – the doctor says you can be fed up well now your temperature is down. Bets, bring the tray down when you want the next course – and don't let Frederick gobble up your soup as well as his!"

That Afternoon

The two ate their soup in a pleasant silence. It was hot and well-flavoured. Fatty took two pieces of toast with it and crunched them up with appetite. He seemed to be hungrier even than Bets!

A distant bark came to their ears. Fatty listened and frowned. "I do think Mother might have let me have Buster in today," he said. "He'd be good for me."

"You didn't want him in yesterday," said Bets, spooning up the last of her soup. "You said his bark would drive you mad."

"Did I really?" said Fatty in surprise. "Fancy my thinking old Buster's bark would ever drive me mad. I think he's got a very nice bark – not too yappy and not too woofy – a proper Scottie bark. I wish you'd ask Mother if I could have him in here this afternoon, Bets. She might do it if you asked her."

"All right. I'll ask her," said Bets, getting up to take the tray. "But I bet she won't let him get on the bed, Fatty. Do you really want some chicken now? I feel a bit full up already."

"Yes. And plenty of bread sauce," said Fatty. "And some more toast. That soup's made me feel warm and comfortable, but it hasn't done much else. Sure you don't want me to carry the tray for you, Bets?"

15

"Idiot," said Bets happily, and walked out with the tray. Mrs. Trotteville was surprised to hear that Fatty really wanted chicken. She filled a plate for him and one for Bets. "The pudding is stewed apple and rice pudding," she said. "He said he wanted two helpings, but I'm sure he won't want even one. There – can you manage, Bets?"

Bets arrived in the bedroom with the tray, and put it down by Fatty's bed. He eyed it with satisfaction. "I'd better get on to that before my appetite fades away," he said, and began to tuck in. Yes, certainly Fatty was on the mend. Nobody could eat like that if they were feeling at all ill!

He slowed down a bit before he reached the end of the chicken and vegetables. "What's the pudding?" he asked Bets.

"Stewed apple and rice," said Bets. Fatty made a face.

"Pooh! What a pudding to plan for some one in bed. It's bad enough to be faced with that when you're up and about. I shan't have any."

"I suppose you're pretending you would have had two enormous helpings if it had been treacle pudding?" suggested Bets, slyly. "You're a fibber, Fatty. You can't eat another thing! Nor can I, as a matter of fact. I'll take this tray down now."

"Don't forget to ask Mother if Buster can come up this afternoon," Fatty called to her.

Bets delivered the tray, broke the news about the lack of appetite for apples and rice, and asked about Buster.

"Well," said Mrs. Trotteville, considering the matter, "well, I wouldn't mind if I thought Frederick would keep quiet, and not get excited with Buster tearing all over the place. Oh, and Bets, your mother said you could stay on to tea if you like. She says Pip has got some one coming to see him this afternoon, and it would be good for you to have a change and be with Frederick for a bit. Would you like to?"

"Oh yes," said Bets. "But doesn't Fatty rest a bit in

the afternoon? I mean – I had to sleep after my dinner when I had 'flu'."

"Yes, certainly he must," said Mrs. Trotteville. "But you needn't stay with him then. You can come down here and have a book to read and then go back again when he is awake. He can bang on the floor or ring the bell when he has had enough sleep. And if he still wants Buster, you can take him up then."

"Oh, good!" said Bets. "I'll just go out into the kitchen and have a word with old Buster, Mrs. Trotteville. He must be missing us all so!"

Buster gave her a frantic welcome. He tore round her on his short legs, rolled over, bounced up again, and altogether behaved as if he was about six months old. He barked non-stop, and the two maids sitting with their cups of tea put their hands up to their ears.

"He's going upstairs to his master this afternoon," said Bets. "Did you hear that, Buster! Going to master!"

Buster thought that Bets meant he was going that very minute. He flung himself at the closed door, and barked madly. Bets laughed. "I'll come and fetch you later on," she said. "In about an hour or so, Buster."

She managed to slide out of the door before Buster could squeeze out too. She left him barking crossly. What! She had gone to see his beloved master, and not taken him, after all her promises? Wuff, wuff, wuff! Grrrrrrr!

Bets went back upstairs to tell Fatty the good news. "I'll settle you down if you like," she said to him. "Then you can go to sleep, and when you wake up, bang on the floor with this stick and I'll come up with Buster. I'm to stay to tea, so we've plenty of time to talk and play games."

"Good," said Fatty, pleased. He was now feeling sleepy and he snuggled down. "But don't go, Bets. There's a nice comfy chair over there, look – and you can borrow one of my Sherlock Holmes stories if you like. There's a pile on that table."

"Your mother said I was to go downstairs and read," said Bets. "I'd better go."

"No, don't," said Fatty. "I don't like being left alone. Stay with me, Bets."

"Don't be silly! You don't care tuppence about being alone – and you'll be asleep in a few moments!" said Bets, with a laugh.

"Bets," said Fatty suddenly, in a voice that made her look across at him in surprise. "Bets, you *must* stay with me! Because of the Voices!"

Bets gaped at him. Voices! Whatever did Fatty mean?

"What Voices?" she said.

"I don't know," said Fatty, still very mysterious. "Sometimes it's a duck, I think. And other times it's a hen. And once it was a dog whining."

Bets was amazed. "What – here in your bedroom?" she asked, disbelievingly. "Fatty, you must have had a very high temperature to think you heard Voices."

"I tell you, there *are* Voices in this bedroom when I'm all alone," said Fatty, leaning up on one elbow. He looked very earnest. "There's a silly old man too, who keeps asking for a cigarette. Bets, do stay with me. If you hear the Voices we could try and find out what they are. Do stay here and sit in that chair. But don't you say a word to Mother, will you? She'll think I've got a temperature or something again."

"All right. I'll stay," said Bets, puzzled and disbelieving. "But I believe you're making it all up, Fatty, just to make me stay here with you. You shouldn't do that."

"Bets, as sure as I lie here, there have been Voices in my room," said Fatty. "Will you believe me, if you hear them? See that duck on the mantelpiece – the china one – well, I've heard it quacking. And see that dog in the picture? He barks and whines!"

"You lie down, Fatty," said Bets, and she pushed him down. "You're dreaming. Or just being silly. I'm going to sit in that chair and read Sherlock Holmes. Don't say another word, or we'll have your mother up here."

Fatty lay down, Bets sat in the chair, wondering why Fatty spoke so much about Voices. She decided that he must have had such a high temperature that he had wandered a little in his mind and heard voices that were not really there. She opened her book and yawned.

Bets fell asleep, and so did Fatty. Except for a log falling in the grate, where a bright fire was burning, there was nothing to be heard. Buster was snoozing in the kitchen, keeping one eye open for the big cat. The cat had to keep a certain distance. One paw over the line and Buster flew at her!

The clock on the mantelpiece ticked on. Half-past two. Three o'clock. It was raining outside, and the afternoon was dark. It would have been too dark for Bets to read if she had been awake. Half-past three. Both Fatty and Bets were perfectly still, and the fire grew rather low.

Then Bets woke up with a jump. She sat up, wondering where she was. Of course – she was in the big chair in Fatty's bedroom! How low the fire was! Fatty must still be asleep, because he hadn't put on his light, and the room was really very dark.

"Quark, quark, quark!"

Bets almost jumped out of her skin. She gazed incredulously at the big china duck on the mantelpiece. Did the quacking come from there? Her heart began to beat fast. Was this one of Fatty's "Voices"? She stared at the duck and thought she saw it move.

"Quark, quark, quark!" There it was again – a rather deep quack, just like the noise made by the drakes on the pond. Bets couldn't believe her eyes.

"Cluck, cuck-cuk-cuk-cuk-cuk-cuk!"

Bets was glued to her chair. There was a hen clucking now – a hen in the bedroom! But how! Why? And now there was a dog whining softly!

She glanced at the picture of the dog but could hardly see it in the darkness. It whined again and gave a little yap.

And then a quavery old voice came from the wardrobe in the far corner.

19

"A cigarette, please, sir. Just a cigarette!"

"Oh, dear," said Bets in fright. "Fatty, Fatty, wake up. Your Voices are here!"

There was a click as Fatty suddenly switched on his bedside light. He sat up in bed, looking at Bets. "Did you hear them too?" he said. "Hark – the old man is beginning again." He pointed over to the wardrobe. Bets looked across at once.

"A cigarette, please, sir. Just a cigarette!"

"I don't like it," said Bets, and she rushed over to Fatty. "I'm frightened. Fatty, what is it?"

"Quark, quark, quark!"

"Cluck, cuk-cuk-cuk-cuk-cuk!"

"Moo-oo-oo-oo!"

"Oh, Fatty, Fatty, what is it?" wept Bets, and covered her face and ears. "Fatty, come out of this room. I'm frightened!"

"Oh, Bets, don't cry! I didn't mean to make you cry," said Fatty, and put an arm round the scared little girl. "I thought you'd guess what it was at once! You are a little silly, Bets, not to guess."

"Guess what?" asked Bets, astonished. She looked up into Fatty's smiling face. "Fatty! It's not just a trick you're doing, is it? What is it?"

"It's a bit of a secret, Bets," said Fatty, putting his mouth to her ear. "I'm practising to be a ventriloquist, that's all. Did you really guess?"

A Lesson in Ventriloquism

Bets could hardly believe her ears. She stared at Fatty's grinning face in amazement.

"But – but – was it you then, making that duck on the mantelpiece quack?" she said. "And that hen cluck, and the dog bark – and that old man ask for a cigarette? It can't be you, Fatty!"

"It is, though," said Fatty. "I've been working at it

all last term. Gosh, the noises that have come from the corners of our dormy each night! And the noises in class too. Once I even got a master to open a cupboard to see if a cat was mewing there."

"But, Fatty – how do you do it?" asked Bets, staring at him. "I've seen ventriloquists on the stage, of course – making their dolls speak – but how do you do it? Fatty, I didn't like it!"

"Now don't you be a silly," said Fatty. "I wouldn't have played the trick on you if I'd thought you were going to be scared. It just shows I must be jolly good. There's no talking duck or hen or dog or old man in this room, Bets, you *must* know that. I wanted to try and see if I could puzzle you – I didn't mean to frighten you. Gosh, I must be a better ventriloquist than I thought!"

A voice came from the wardrobe again – or at least Bets *thought* it did!

"A cigarette, please, sir – just a cigarette!"

Bets looked swiftly round at Fatty and this time she laughed. "Oh, Fatty – you're clever – but I just saw your throat moving when you said that. How do you manage to throw your voice somewhere else, though? Fatty, it's marvellous! Whatever will the others say!"

Fatty sat himself comfortably up in bed. "Well," he began, "I'll tell you a bit about it, Bets. A chap came down to our school last term to entertain us. He was a ventriloquist and he had a couple of idiotic-looking dolls, whose heads could turn from side to side. Their eyes could open and shut, and their mouths worked up and down. You've seen a ventriloquist, haven't you? Well, he was absolutely super, this chap. I honestly couldn't see either his mouth or his throat working in even the smallest movement – and yet it was his own voice that made those dolls seem to talk – and sing too!"

"Yes. I think ventriloquists are marvellous too," said Bets. "I haven't the faintest idea how they do it. But *you* must know, Fatty, because you can ventil – ventrilo. . . ."

"Ventriloquise," said Fatty. "Well, I do know a *bit*

21

"Oh, Fatty, Fatty, what is it?" cried Bets

now. But I've had to get it out of books, because you can't learn interesting and really useful things like ventriloquism – or conjuring – or disguising yourself – at school. Such a pity they don't have things like that in the time-table. Wouldn't I work at them!"

"Yes. So would I," said Bets. "Did you have to practise ventriloquism yourself, then, Fatty, with nobody to help you?"

"Yes," said Fatty. "But it's difficult to be anywhere by yourself at school, you know, so I had to let a few of the boys into the secret. We've got about six ventriloquists at my school now."

"But you're the best, I bet you are, Fatty," said Bets, at once.

Fatty wished he could say he was. But honesty compelled him to admit that another boy was better than he was.

"We've got a black boy at our school," he said. "A Zulu Prince, or something. He's the best. But that's not to be wondered at, because apparently all his uncles and great uncles and grandfathers were able to throw their voices wherever they wanted to. It's an old talent with Zulus, apparently. Anyway, when he knew I was trying to learn to throw my voice, he showed me a few tricks."

"Tell me, Fatty," begged Bets. "What tricks?"

"Well," said Fatty, banging his pillows and settling himself comfortably, "first of all, I'll explain the name ventriloquism. It comes from two words – venter, which means tummy, and loqui, which means to speak – in other words a ventriloquist was supposed to be a man who could speak by using his tummy in some way."

"Do you use *your* tummy then?" asked Bets. "If so, you ought to have a jolly fine ventriloquist voice."

"Don't be rude," said Fatty, with dignity. "As a matter of fact, the people who thought that, made a mistake. The tummy is *not* used."

"Oh. What is, then?" asked Bets, intensely interested.

"Well," said Fatty, "as far as I can see, a ventriloquist

23

forms his words in the ordinary way – but he lets his breath escape very slowly indeed – and he closes up his glottis – his throat – as much as he can, and opens his mouth as little as possible – oh, and he only uses the tip of his tongue."

Bets couldn't follow this, but she didn't much mind as she had no intention of becoming a ventriloquist herself. She was quite sure she would be no good at it at all. The whole thing sounded quite impossible to do. But Fatty, as usual, had tackled the impossible and done it!

"You *are* clever, Fatty," she said. "Now do some more ventriloquism and let me see how you do it."

But she couldn't see, of course, except that Fatty's throat moved a little, and once his lips moved too. "Just a cigarette, please, just a cigarette," came a quavering voice which didn't appear to be anywhere near Fatty at all. She instinctively looked over to the wardrobe again. Fatty was looking there too, as if somebody was really there.

"It's queer," said Bets. "Really queer. How do you throw your voice like that, Fatty?"

"I don't really. You just think I do, and you look at the place where you imagine the voice is coming from, and hear it there," said Fatty. "That's just a trick, of course. Though this Zulu chap I was telling you about can *really* throw his voice, it seems to me. Anyway, one day it sounded to us as if there was somebody calling us from outside the classroom door – but when we went to see, there wasn't any one in sight – and old Boobanti was sitting in his chair inside the room, grinning away like anything. 'I fool English boys, I fool English,' he kept saying."

"I wish I went to your school," said Bets. "You always make it sound so exciting, Fatty. Fancy you being a ventriloquist now – whatever will you be next?"

"Well, you just never know when things like that will help you," said Fatty. "It might come in very useful with my detective work when I'm grown-up. It's a jolly amusing trick, anyhow."

24

There came the sound of excited barking, and the thump of leaping feet on the stairs.

"Buster," said Fatty. "Gosh, in all this excitement about my ventriloquist act, we'd forgotten about poor old Buster. Bets, don't say a word to mother about my ventriloquist stunt."

Before Bets could assure Fatty that she certainly wouldn't, the door opened and in came Mrs. Trotteville with a tremendously excited Buster rushing in front. He leapt straight on to the bed, of course, and flung himself on Fatty. He put his paws up on the boy's shoulders and proceeded to lick him all over the face, barking loudly.

"Mercy, Buster, mercy!" begged Fatty, and disappeared completely under the bed-clothes to escape the excited dog. Buster followed at once, and a curious heaving earthquake formed itself in the bed, accompanied by yells and barks.

"Frederick! Buster must come out!" cried Mrs. Trotteville. "Oh, dear, neither of them can hear me. FATTY! BUSTER! FATTY!"

Fatty appeared eventually, his hair towsled, his eyes bright, holding Buster in such a tight grip that the dog couldn't move even a leg.

"What do you do with mad dogs, Mother?" he asked. "Honestly, he's quite dippy."

"Oh, Frederick — put him down outside the bed," said Mrs. Trotteville. "That's right, Buster. If you dare to get on the bed again I'll set the cat on you."

"Wuff," barked Buster rudely. "Wuff to that!"

"Frederick, listen," said his mother. "It's almost tea-time. You can get up, put on your dressing-gown, and stay up for two hours. You can have tea while you're up. Bets can go and get it in ten minutes' time."

She went out of the room, and Buster immediately leapt up on to the bed again. But this time he was not so uproarious. He had given Fatty the welcome he had been saving up for him, now he was content to lie by him, licking his hand whenever it came near his black nose.

25

Bets got Fatty's dressing-gown and slippers, and put the arm-chair in front of the fire. Fatty got out of bed. At first he meant to leap out, but somehow his legs failed to obey his orders. He found that his knees were still very shaky.

"Are you going to tell the others about your ventriloquism?" asked Bets. "Will you teach them too?"

"No, I shan't teach them," said Fatty. "The difficulty is not so much the *learning*, Bets, it's the practising. You make all kinds of queer noises then, and people don't like it."

"No. I can't see Mother being very pleased if Pip tried to learn," said Bets. "She says he's noisy enough already. Anyway, his school report wasn't very good. She and Daddy would be sure to think it was messing about with ventriloquism that made him not work hard at his class subjects."

"Pity," said Fatty, beginning on the buttered toast. "Is there any honey to go with the toast? I always think hot, buttery toast and honey make a jolly good pair – but usually you get one without the other. No – there's no honey. Be a pet and go and ask for some, Bets. Don't be too long, or else the honey won't be needed."

"Why not?" said Bets, surprised.

"Because there won't be any toast left to go with it," said Fatty. "Go on, hurry!"

"You really are a greedy pig, Fatty," said Bets. "Don't dare to eat it all! I never in my life saw such lovely drippy toast – it's just swimming in butter!"

She went out to get the honey. Fatty looked down at Buster, who was sitting beside him, looking up adoringly, his mouth open and his tongue hanging out because of the heat of the fire. Fatty tipped up a piece of buttery toast and let two or three drops of the melted butter drip down to Buster's pink tongue. Buster was agreeably surprised. He swallowed twice and then held out his tongue again.

"Quark, quark, quark," said Fatty, down in his throat. Buster looked at him inquiringly and wagged his tail.

"Cluck-cuk-cuk-cuk-cuk," clucked Fatty. "Where's that hen, Buster, where is it?"

Buster thumped his tail on the ground. But he didn't go and look for either duck or hen.

"Too sensible, aren't you?" said Fatty, with his mouth full. "No matter where I pretend the sounds come from, you jolly well know they're made by *me*, don't you? Quark, quark, quark!"

Mr. Goon hears Strange Voices

In three days' time all the Find-Outers were apparently completely themselves again. Perhaps a spurt of brilliantly fine weather had something to do with it. All of them felt that they must be out in the sunshine, however cold it was otherwise.

They went for their first walk together that holiday, enjoying the stroll, though only Bets really felt like running. "I vote we pop into the dairy and have a hot cup of chocolate," said Fatty, as they turned into the High Street. "Come on, Buster, it's no use staring at cats that are safely sitting on walls. They won't come down for you to chase them! Funny that a clever dog like you shouldn't have learnt that elementary fact yet!"

They went into the little dairy and sat down at one of the tables there. In the summer they had ice-cold milk there, and ice-creams, or lemonade. In the winter the little shop did a roaring trade in hot milk, cocoa, and hot chocolate.

A short, plump woman came to serve them. "Well, well," she said, beaming at them. "I thought you must have gone back to school. I've not seen you for so long. What would you like?"

"Hot chocolate, ginger biscuits, and currant buns, please," said Fatty. He drew a handful of change out of his pocket to pay. Fatty always had plenty of money!

"I'll pay," said Larry. "I've not spent half my Christmas money yet. You're always paying out for us!"

Fatty let him pay. He knew that it often made Larry feel embarrassed when he so often had to allow him, Fatty, to pay for their treats. Anyway, Fatty could always pay for the second round of chocolate and biscuits! "Flu seems to have enlarged my appetite," he said. "I've not stopped feeling hungry for two days."

"Only because you jolly well know you're going to get plenty to eat," said Pip. "It wouldn't be any fun being hungry if you thought there wasn't going to be even a bit of bread to chew for days!"

Nobody could think of an answer to that remark. Buster suddenly got up and went to the door. He barked loudly.

"Be quiet!" said Fatty. "Behave yourself, Buster. Don't bark at that dear old lady."

"He's not," said Bets suddenly, peering through the shop window from where she sat. "It's Mr. Goon."

"Well, I hope he keeps out of here," said Pip, beginning on a currant bun. "I say, these are good – new as anything."

Bets let her eyes wander round the shop. Up on the mantelpiece was a model of a cow, standing about two feet high. It had a head that would nod up and down if any one set it going. She got up and went over to it.

"I like this cow," she said. "I'll set its head nid-nodding. Let's see if it manages to nod it all the time we're here."

She set the head nodding and went back to her chair, watching the cow. Buster began to bark again, and the five swung their heads round to the door.

Mr. Goon was standing there, looking so plump that the buttons on his tunic were stretched to bursting-point. "Call this dog to you," he commanded Fatty. "Put him on a lead. I won't have him dancing round my ankles."

"Why? Are you coming to have a drink of hot milk or something?" asked Fatty. He deftly put Buster on the lead, and made him sit down. Fatty was hoping against hope that Mr. Goon was indeed coming to sit

28

in the shop and have a drink. Fatty had a bright idea, and wanted to carry it out!

Mr. Goon stalked in and sat down at the table next but one to the five children's. He called for a cup of cocoa and a bun.

"Cold outside for you again, isn't it, Mr. Goon, sir?" said the short plump woman, setting down a cup of cocoa and a bun in front of the red-faced policeman.

Mr. Goon took no notice of her. He glanced across at the children. "Ho – seems like I've had a nice quiet time these holidays," he began. "No nosey-parkering, no Interfering with the Law. That says something for the 'flu', that does. You must have felt funny not being able to stick your noses in a mystery."

Nobody answered. Fatty spoke a few words to Larry, and Larry said a few back. Nobody looked at Mr. Goon. He didn't like being ignored. He raised his voice.

"Or have you got a mystery on hand?" he began again. "A nice juicy mystery to make a mess of?"

Fatty looked at him. "Now how did you hear *that*, Mr. Goon?" he said, in a surprised voice. "Larry, have you been saying anything about our latest mystery?"

Larry rose immediately to Fatty's invitation to be absurd.

"Which case do you mean?" he said. "The mystery of the red-nosed reindeer, or the one about the flying saucers? We've solved them both, haven't we?"

"Oh yes. I didn't mean *those*," said Fatty. "Mr. Goon probably knows all about those by now. They're stale news, aren't they, Mr. Goon. No, Larry – I meant the Mystery of the Strange Voices."

"Gah!" said Mr. Goon, biting violently into his bun. "Strange voices – you don't know what you're talking about. Lot of silly make-up!"

The other four had pricked up their ears when they heard Fatty refer to Strange Voices. They all knew about his ventriloquial powers now, and he had practised a few of his tricks in front of them. Why had he mentioned Strange Voices to Mr. Goon?

"Lot of silly make-up," said Mr. Goon again, and

took a sip of hot cocoa. "Strange voices! Gah!"

"Oh yes – that mystery's not solved yet, is it?" said Larry, speaking to Fatty in a voice loud enough for Mr. Goon to hear. "Curious case that – people hearing strange voices which aren't really there. Somebody casting a spell on them, I suppose."

"Baby-talk," said Mr. Goon, drinking his cocoa rather loudly.

"You may be right," said Fatty seriously. "But believe it or not, some people lately have been hearing ducks quack where there are no ducks, hens clucking, and people speaking – and yet there don't seem to be any there."

"You'll tell me that cow on the mantelpiece will start to moo next," said Mr. Goon, swallowing the last of the currant bun. Fatty scribbled something quickly on a piece of paper and pushed it across the table to the others.

"Cow will moo," he had written. "But none of you is to hear it."

Mr. Goon wiped his mouth. "Quacking ducks, clucking hens, mooing cows," he observed sarcastically. "Silly make-up. Bosh and rubbish!"

"It's a nice cow, isn't it," said Bets, looking across at it. "Its head is still going up and down."

Mr. Goon looked across at it too.

"Moo-oo, moo-oo, moo-oo," said the cow, mooing in exact time to the nodding of its head. The mooing was so realistic, and so exactly in time to the nodding, that even the children, with the exception of Fatty, thought for one moment that the mooing noise did actually come from it.

Mr. Goon stared at the cow, astounded. He glanced round at the children. Not one of them, of course, took any notice of the mooing, remembering Fatty's hastily scribbled instructions. They lifted up their cups and drank, Bets hoping to goodness that she wouldn't start to giggle.

Mr. Goon looked at the nodding cow again. It had

stopped mooing – principally because Fatty had been overcome with an urge to laugh. But, as Goon looked at it, it gave such a large and unexpected moo that the policeman jumped violently. Then the mooing quietened and went on in time with the nodding of the animal's head.

Mr. Goon swallowed hard. "Moo-oo, moo-oo, moo-oo," went the cow, nodding its head. Nobody would ever have believed that it was merely Fatty throwing the noise across to the mantelpiece!

Mr. Goon felt rather sick. He didn't know what to make of it at all. He looked at the children again. They were taking absolutely no notice at all of the mooing cow. Neither was Buster, of course. Was it possible that they were not hearing what Mr. Goon was hearing?

The little plump woman came bustling into the shop with some more buns for the children. The cow stopped mooing. Mr. Goon cleared his throat and spoke to the shop-woman.

"Er – nice cow that of yours, my good woman – the one on the mantelpiece, I mean. Very life-like? You'd almost expect it to moo!"

"You will have your joke, sir," said the little woman. "My, if I heard it moo I'd think there was something wrong with me. I'd think I was going crazy!"

"That's just what we were saying," said Fatty gravely. "Strange Voices are about – people are hearing them. What are they? A Warning? Brrrrrr! I'm glad *I* don't hear them!"

"Well, we live in queer days, no doubt about it," said the little shop-woman puzzled, and hurried off again. The cow began to moo once more, but so softly that Mr. Goon was not absolutely sure if he was hearing it or not. Could he be imagining it? He gazed so earnestly at the nodding cow that Bets felt an irresistible giggle rising up from the very middle of her tummy. She knew from experience that they were the worst kind of giggles – the ones that heaved up and broke out helplessly.

"Talk, do talk," she besought the others in a low voice. "I'm going to laugh."

31

All but Fatty talked in low voices, saying any non-sense that came into their heads. Fatty stopped making the cow moo. Mr. Goon sat back cautiously. Thank goodness the cow was behaving normally now. Maybe his ears had just played him a trick.

"Quark, quark, quark!" Mr. Goon jumped violently again, and looked all round. That was a duck quacking, not a doubt of it.

QUARK! Mr. Goon's eyes caught sight of a wild duck, beautifully stuffed, placed in a glass case at the end of the shop. He gazed at it, holding his breath.

"Quark, quark, QUARK!" The duck appeared to be looking at him out of its glass eye, and its half-open beak seemed to be quacking. Mr. Goon leapt up, full of horror.

"That duck!" he said wildly. "Did you hear it!"

"What duck?" asked Larry. "Oh, Mr. Goon – surely – surely you are not suggesting that the duck in the glass case is quacking!"

"Mr. Goon – don't say you are hearing the Strange Voices!" said Fatty, earnestly and solemnly.

"Quark!" The noise seemed to come from some-where behind Mr. Goon. He gave a loud, hunted cry and ran from the shop, Buster almost tripping him up with his lead. And then the children collapsed over the table, crying tears of laughter into their empty cups. "Mr. Goon, Mr. Goon, you couldn't have been fun-nier!"

Something Happens at Last

"Oh, Fatty – HOW do you do it?" said Daisy, mopping her eyes and feeling very weak. "The way you made that cow moo in time to its nodding was perfect. Honestly, I could have believed myself that the thing was mooing."

"So would I," said Bets. "Oh, dear – don't do that sort of thing too often, Fatty – I simply shan't be able to keep my giggles down if you do. Mr. Goon's face! His eyes almost fell out of his head!"

"He must be feeling pretty puzzled," said Larry. "I bet he'll wake up at night and hear noises that aren't there!"

They paid their second bill and went out. What a pity there wasn't any first-class mystery to probe into! These were the first holidays in which nothing of any sort or kind had turned up. And there were only a few days left.

"Can't we spoof old Goon a bit, just to get some kind of excitement into our last few days?" said Larry. "That laugh did me more good than a dozen days in bed!"

"Me too," said Pip. "I was feeling rather low this morning, but now I'm feeling fine. That's obviously what we all want – a jolly good laugh every now and again."

"And Fatty's the one to give it to us," said Bets, squeezing his arm. "Fatty, do let's see if we can't spoof Mr. Goon a bit?"

"But how?" said Fatty. "I mean – we can't follow him around with all kinds of noises. He'd soon begin to associate them with us. If every time he hears a cow moo or a duck quack, or hears mysterious voices going on, and sees us somewhere near, well, even *he's* wide-awake enough to put two and two together – us and the noises."

"I suppose you're right," said Bets, with a sigh, putting away her visions of pursuing Mr. Goon with strange and wonderful sounds. "Well – perhaps something will happen to give us a bit of excitement."

It was queer that she said that – because that very night something did happen, though nothing very startling. They didn't know about it till the next morning.

The milkman told Larry. "Heard about the break-in at the Cedars last night?" he said. "It's next door but one from you. It's a small house, and a man called Mr. Fellows has rented it since a week or two. Lived there all alone."

"What happened?" said Larry.

33

"Well, apparently somebody broke in, and rifled the house from top to bottom," said the milkman. "We don't know if Mr. Fellows was there or not – anyway, he's gone this morning. Hasn't come back yet either."

"Who discovered this?" asked Larry, quite excited to think that all this had taken place so near to his own home. Why, he might have heard something in the night – a shout, the breaking of a window, or something. Alas, he had been too sound asleep.

"I found the house-door open, and a window broken at the back, when I took the milk early this morning," said the milkman. "I peeped in at the hall-door and my, what a mess the place was in! I stepped in and telephoned for the police at once."

"Oh – did Mr. Goon come?" asked Larry, disappointed. He had hoped for one moment that the Find-Outers might get in first! It was still early, only just after breakfast-time.

"Yes. He's there now – taking notes and looking for finger-prints and the rest of it," said the milkman. "He's feeling important this morning. Told me to keep my big mouth shut and not tell any one what I found – after I'd told every single one of my customers! What does he think I am – a clam?"

"Did you notice anything at all out of the way?" asked Larry.

"Nothing," said the milkman. "I didn't stop to look round, anyway, I telephoned the police at once. Mustn't disturb anything, you know, in cases like this."

Larry got on his bicycle and went to tell Fatty. It might be nothing, or it might be something interesting, you never knew. Fatty would soon get the old brains to work and decide if the Find-Outers were to do anything or not!

Fatty was most interested. "This cheers me up immensely," he said. "It may be a potty little robbery, but we'd better go and find out. If the house really *was* rifled from top to bottom, it looks as though some one was trying very hard to find something of great importance to him. What was it – and who was it?"

They collected Pip and Bets, fetched Daisy, and all five of them, with Buster, went up to the house that stood two doors from Larry's. It didn't look as if any one was there. Mr. Goon must have come and gone. Good.

"Now then," said Fatty. "Examine all the paths and beds round the house. Look for the usual things – foot-marks, cigarette ends, hand-prints on window-ledges, etc. Make notes of what you find, and we'll compare later."

"Aren't you coming with us?" asked Bets, seeing Fatty turn away.

"No. I'm going to look in at the windows and see if there's anything interesting inside," said Fatty.

But the curtains were drawn across and he couldn't see anything. He went steadily round the little house, but not one window could he see into. The front door was closed and fastened now, and the back door was locked too.

Fatty came to the broken window at the back. It was the kitchen window. Obviously the robber or whatever he was, had got in here. Fatty stuck his hand inside and moved the curtain. The kitchen was upside down! Drawers had been pulled from the dresser and from the table. Cupboards were open and their contents dragged out on to the floor! What could the intruder have been looking for?

Fatty suddenly heard a sound inside the kitchen. He listened. What was it? He heard it again, and then peep-ing in at the window once more, he made out two gleam-ing eyes looking at him from a cupboard.

"Miaow! Miaow!" said the owner of the eyes piteously.

"Gosh – it's a kitten," said Fatty. "Scared to death, I expect, and nobody to feed it or care for it, poor little thing!"

The others came round the corner of the house, note-books in their hands. "Here!" said Fatty, beckoning. "There's a kitten left in the house! What shall we do?"

"Get it," said Daisy promptly.

35

"How?" asked Pip. "All the doors and windows are shut tight. We've checked that."

"This one's broken," said Fatty. "If I wrap my hand in a handkerchief I think I could put it through the broken pane and do what the thief did – undo the clasp and open the window. Then I could get in and rescue the kitten."

"Well, go on then," said Larry, looking all round. "There's no one about. Goon won't come back yet."

Fatty took out a big white handkerchief. He twisted it firmly round his fingers. Then he gingerly put his hand through the hole in the broken pane and tried to reach the fastening of the window. It was a casement, opening sideways once the clasp was moved.

"Got it," said Fatty, and jerked the clasp. It slid down stiffly and he took back his hand again. He could now easily open the window.

"Done it," he said pleased, and hopped up to the ledge. Buster began to bark, wanting to go with Fatty.

"Keep him quiet, for goodness' sake," said Fatty. "We don't want any one to see me climbing in!"

They hushed Buster while Fatty climbed nimbly into the kitchen. He found the tiny kitten, which crouched back in the cupboard, spitting and scared. But it soon began purring when Fatty picked it up and petted it.

"I'll find some milk," he called quietly to the others. "I expect it's hungry."

He came to the larder and looked inside. Even that was untidy, and a broken dish lay on the tiled floor. Fancy hunting in the larder too! Whatever had the intruder been after?

"Here you are, kitty," said Fatty, and put down a saucer of milk for the little creature. It lapped hungrily. When it had finished it rubbed itself against Fatty's legs, purring. He bent to pick it up, but it scurried away, and ran through the doorway into the hall.

"Puss, puss!" called Fatty. "Come back here."

"What's up?" said Pip's voice, looking in at the window. "Daisy says if you hand the kitten out to her she'll take it home, as she lives so near. They've got a kitten too, and it can be with hers till somebody comes back here."

"Right. But I'll have to find it first," said Fatty. "It's dashed through the kitchen door into the hall. Half a tick. I'll get it. I can hear it there somewhere."

He went out of the kitchen door into the hall. He paused there, amazed at the untidiness. Coats, shoes, umbrellas were all in wild confusion on the floor, flung there from the hall-cupboard and from a chest of drawers.

The kitten was nowhere to be seen. Fatty went into one room after another, but the little thing was hiding, whether from fright or from play he didn't know.

Fatty took the opportunity of having a good look round. There were three rooms downstairs and three above and a bathroom. Each of them was in confusion. By the soot that lay in the fire-places Fatty guessed that the hunter had even felt up the chimney for whatever it was that he had been looking for.

And then, as he came out from a bedroom on to the little landing, Fatty saw something in a corner, near the top of the stairs. It was bright red. He picked it up.

"A child's glove," he said to himself. "A very *small* glove, for a very small child. But surely there was no child here? And there's only one glove. Could Mr. Fellows have been hiding a child here – kidnapped it, perhaps – and the other fellow came to find it?"

He shook his head. "No – people don't look for even very small children up chimneys and in drawers. I wonder whether there are any more clothes for a child here. It doesn't look like a house where children came at all – not a single toy, not a book or a doll – and no cot."

There were no children's clothes to be seen, thrown in the muddle on the floor. All kinds of other clothes were there – men's coats, trousers, vests, shoes, hats – as well as a trouser-press flung down and opened, books, cushions, papers, blankets, sheets, pillow-cases. . . .

"Well," said Fatty, slipping the child's red glove into his pocket. "I'll keep it, just in case – though in case of what I don't know! Only *one* of the pair – that's the

37

queer part. Was a child here last night – and was it dressed in a hurry, so that it dropped one glove? No, it couldn't be."

A loud whisper penetrated to him.

"Fatty! Quick! Goon's coming back. He's coming up the road. QUICK, Fatty!"

Mr. Goon is Astounded

Almost before Fatty had had time to get downstairs there came the sound of Goon's angry voice.

"Now then, you kids! What are you doing here? Clear orf!"

Then came the sound of Buster's barking. Fatty grinned. How many, many times had this same scene been acted – the Find-Outers snooping round – Goon finding them – ordered them off – and Buster objecting loudly! Well – Buster could certainly look after not only himself, but all the children too.

Fatty wondered whether he could slip out of the front door. He could hear that Mr. Goon was round at the back.

"Interfering with the Law!" he heard, in the policeman's angry voice. "Poking your noses in! What's it to do with you, I'd like to know. Clear orf!"

"Well, we live just close by," said Larry. "It's naturally interesting to us – to Daisy and me, I mean. If burglars are in the district I want to get some information in case they come to rob our house too, next door but one."

"Gah!" said Goon disbelievingly. "Tommy-rot! Just an excuse for interfering. This here job's a potty little job – no mystery in it at all. Not worth your notice, see – And take that dog away before I lose my temper with him. Nasty yappy little mongrel!"

Fatty longed to be out there with the others. Calling Buster a *mongrel*! Why, the little Scottie had a pedigree a yard long, and all his grandparents had been champions. Fatty boiled with rage. He tiptoed to the front door. He didn't want Mr. Goon to catch him in the house, even though he had the perfectly good excuse to offer of rescuing the kitten.

"Where's that fat boy?" demanded Mr. Goon, suddenly realizing that Fatty was absent. "Still in bed with the 'flu', I hope. Best place for him, too. Hope he gets a relapse! WILL you call this dog off?"

Larry called Buster. "Buster, come here. I can find some better ankles for you if you want some."

Mr. Goon snorted. That was one of the things he did remarkably well. "Go on out of this garden, all of you," he said. "Any more messing about here and I'll report you. Yes, and I'll go round to your parents again, too – specially yours, Master Philip Hilton!"

Pip hastily removed himself from the garden of the little house, taking Bets with him. He didn't want Goon to make any more complaints to his parents. They had a habit of taking Mr. Goon seriously! Larry and Daisy followed, Larry holding Buster by the collar. They stood outside the front gate, wondering what Fatty was going to do.

Fatty was most unfortunate. He opened the front door from inside at exactly the same moment that Mr. Goon unlocked it from the outside. Mr. Goon stared at Fatty as if a thunderbolt had hit him. His mouth fell open and he went a familiar purple colour. He swallowed hard.

"Good morning, Mr. Goon," said Fatty, smoothly. "Do come in. I'll shut the door for you."

Mr. Goon stepped in, still wordless. Then he exploded into speech.

"What you doing here? HERE, in this house that's under police supervision. You want to get locked up, I suppose – Being Found on Enclosed Premises, and up to no good, I'll be bound! HO!"

Fatty stepped back out of range of Mr. Goon's explosions. "I heard a kitten mewing here," he said. still politely. "And being a subscriber to the R.S.P.C.A. –

39

"Any more messing about and I'll report you"

if you know what that means, Mr. Goon – I naturally had to come into the house to find it."

"Pah!" said Mr. Goon, disbelievingly. "This here house is habsolutely hempty! I've been through it meself with a tooth-comb already!"

"This 'ere 'ouse hisn't habsolutely hempty," said Fatty. "Dear me, I seem to be getting muddled. Hark, Mr. Goon – can't you hear the kitten mewing now?"

"Miaow!" said the kitten, and obligingly crept out from under the hall-stand. It went to Fatty and rubbed affectionately against his legs. Then it looked at Mr. Goon, hissed at him and spat.

"Most intelligent behaviour," observed Fatty. "I hope you believe in the kitten now, Mr. Goon."

Mr. Goon did. He had to. "Take it away and take yourself off too," he said to Fatty. "I've work to do here. And Keep Out of This, see?"

"You'll be careful of the dog here, won't you, Mr. Goon," said Fatty. "I'm not quite sure where it is – you may possibly hear it growling somewhere, and trace it by that."

"There's no dog here," said Mr. Goon, stalking past Fatty. "A kitten I might have missed, being so small like, but not a dog. What do you take me for?"

"It would be better not to tell you," murmured Fatty. "Not here, anyway."

He was just behind the policeman, and it was as well for Mr. Goon that he couldn't see the innocent expression on Fatty's face – a look that all his form-masters knew only too well.

A blood-curdling growl suddenly came from somewhere in the house. Mr. Goon stopped as if he had been shot. "What's that?" he said.

"Sounded like the dog," said Fatty. "What a horrible animal it must be. I think I'll go, Mr. Goon, and leave you to tackle him."

Another growl came from somewhere, and the policeman took two hurried steps backwards, treading heavily on Fatty's foot.

"Ouch!" said Fatty. "Look out where you're going if
41

you want to walk backwards, Mr. Goon! Well – good-bye – I'll leave you now."

"You come and help me find that dog," said Mr. Goon, changing his mind completely about wanting Fatty to clear off. "It might want two of us to get him. Funny I didn't see him or hear him when I was here before this morning."

Fatty grinned behind Mr. Goon's broad back. He debated whether to produce another animal-noise. This ventriloquism was Most Useful!

"All right, Mr. Goon," he said. "If you think it's my duty to stay and help you, I will. I'm always around when Duty Calls, you know."

Mr. Goon was very thankful. He began to tiptoe forward into the little dining-room. Fatty followed a few paces behind. He suddenly gave a shout that made Goon nearly fall over backwards.

"Look, look – what's that – over there! LOOK OUT!"

Mr. Goon was so anxious to get out as well as to look out that he almost fell over Fatty, trying to rush out of the room. Fatty clutched him as he went.

"It's all right! It's all right! I just caught sight of you in that mirror over there, Mr. Goon, and it was such a dreadful sight I thought it must be some one lying in wait for us. Gosh, thank goodness it was only your reflection!"

Mr. Goon was very angry and very relieved. He glared at Fatty. "Any more of this funny business," he began, and then stopped suddenly.

From somewhere behind came the sound of heavy grunting. Mr. Goon swung round at once. "Did you hear that?" he asked Fatty, breathlessly. "That grunting noise. What was it? It sounded out there in the hall."

"Yes, it did," said Fatty, clutching at Mr. Goon's arm and making him jump again. "You go first, Mr. Goon. I'm scared."

So was Mr. Goon. He tiptoed into the hall and promptly fell over the kitten which made a dart at him as soon as he appeared. He retreated into the dining-room again, bumping into Fatty. The grunting noise was heard once more, this time sounding farther off.

"It's a pig!" said Mr. Goon, hardly able to believe his ears. "Sounded upstairs that time. Did you think it was a pig, Master Frederick?"

The more frightened and puzzled Mr. Goon became, the more polite he got. At this rate, thought Fatty, he'll soon be bowing to me every time he speaks! He badly wanted to laugh, but he firmly thrust down the ever-mounting guffaw that wanted to rise up and explode.

"What sort of a fellow was it who lived here, Mr. Goon?" asked Fatty, innocently. "Was he fond of ani-mals? He seems to have kept kittens, and dogs, and pigs, anyway."

"How was it I didn't see the pig when I was here this morning," marvelled Goon. "I turned everything over and looked everywhere for clues. And yet I didn't see the dog or the pig. Shall we go upstairs to find the pig?"

"Yes. But be careful the dog doesn't rush out at you," said Fatty. "You go first, Mr. Goon."

Mr. Goon didn't want to go first. He pushed Fatty in front of him, and then immediately wished he hadn't because a deep and ferocious growl came from some-where behind him. Fatty was certainly practising his new talent well!

And then a new sound came to worry poor Mr. Goon. A voice came from somewhere, a groaning voice that said:

"I never did it, I never! Ooooooh! I never did it! Where's my auntie?"

Goon listened, petrified. He began to feel as if he was in a nightmare. He whispered to Fatty. "There's a man here somewhere! This beats all! We'd better get help. I'm not going to snoop round here with dogs, and pigs, and a man groaning. What's been happening since I was here this morning?"

"Look, you stay here, Mr. Goon, and I'll go and get help," said Fatty, and moved firmly into the hall. But Mr. Goon clutched at him.

"No, don't leave me here alone. Can't *you* stay while I get help?"

"Remember your duty, Mr. Goon," said Fatty solemnly. "There is Something Queer here, and it's your duty to examine it. But it's not *my* duty. I'll go and get help. Good-bye!"

Goon held on to him tightly, and then the Voice began again. "I never did it, I never! Oooooooh! I never did it! Where's my auntie?"

Goon began to shake. "What's he mean, talking about his auntie?" he whispered. "Come on, let's go! This is a mad-house, this is."

"Mr. Goon – why not telephone for help!" said Fatty, suddenly catching sight of the telephone in the hall. "You'd get some one here in a trice then."

Mr. Goon was so relieved at this bright idea of Fatty's that he almost embraced him. He stumbled to the telephone and dialled a number.

Fatty heard him telephoning to another constable. He tiptoed silently out of the front door, grinning as he heard Goon's agonized voice.

"Send some one up here at once. There's a fierce dog in the house – and a pig – yes, I said a pig – P-I-G. Yes, PIG, you ass. And a groaning man who wants his Auntie. AUNTIE! Yes, I did say Auntie. Are you deaf, or something? Well, how do *I* know why he wants his Auntie? No, I'm not daft, but I soon shall be if you don't send some one to this address at once. Yes – I do want help – YES, there IS a dog here – and a pig – and an Auntie – no, not an Auntie, but a man who wants one. Oh, and there's a kitten, too, I forgot to mention that."

There was a pause as Goon listened to a few remarks from the other end of the telephone. He splutted into it again.

"Any more sauce from you, Kenton, and I'll report you. I'm NOT having a joke with you. You come up here at once. AT ONCE, do you hear?"

Fatty heard all this and felt that he really must go somewhere and laugh. He tiptoed round to the back of

44

the house where there was a shed he could go into and laugh in peace. He saw the broken casement window, hanging open, as he passed. He thrust his head inside, and sent a terrible growl into the house.

Mr. Goon heard it. He looked round, and found that Fatty had gone. He was alone – alone in the house with a host of terrifying things. It was too much for Goon. He fled at top speed out of the front door, and didn't stop running till he came to the bottom of the road.

Fatty heard him go. And then he laughed. How he laughed! It really was the best laugh Fatty had ever had in all his life!

Laughter is Good for the 'Flu'!

Fatty's laughter echoed across the next garden and came to the ears of the others. They had retreated to Larry's house, and had made their way into the back garden to wait for Fatty. Buster heard the laughter too, and pricked up his ears. He began to bark delightedly. Like every one else, he loved Fatty's enormous laughter!

Larry climbed up on to the wall. He gave the piercing whistle that the Find-Outers sometimes used. Fatty heard it and saw Larry.

"Wait for me! I'm coming!" he called. He was soon in the garden with the others. They retired to a little out-house at the bottom of the garden.

"What happened? And why did Goon rush out of the house so suddenly at top speed?" asked Daisy. "We saw him flashing by the gate like dark-blue lightning!"

Fatty began to laugh helplessly again. The others had to laugh as they watched him. Pip gave him a punch and Buster leapt on him in excitement. Why was his master so pleased?

"Come on – tell us the joke," said Pip.

So Fatty told them, and soon they were all helplessly sitting on the floor of the out-house, holding their sides, picturing Mr. Goon's amazement at the thought of the grunting pig, the growling dog, and the groaning man.

"That Auntie bit! Oh, what made you think of that?" groaned Larry, holding his aching sides. "That's a touch of genius. Oh dear – only an idiot like Goon would have taken all that in! I say – what *will* Inspector Jenks think when Goon makes out a report full of pigs, and dogs, and men that want their aunties?"

That made them all laugh again, but Fatty began to look a little more sober. He rubbed his nose thoughtfully. "I hadn't thought of Goon making out a report," he said. "Yes, I suppose he'll have to. Gosh, the Chief Inspector will smell a rat, I should think. Especially if he knows I was with Goon at the time all this happened."

"He may not put you into the report," said Daisy, comfortingly. "He'd leave you out if. he possibly could. He hates admitting you are ever on the same job as he is."

"He telephoned for help," said Fatty. "Let's go and see if he's met his help and if they're coming back."

Just as they got to the front gate and hung over it, with Buster doing his best to squeeze underneath, Mr. Goon came up the road with P.C. Kenton. P.C. Kenton had been most astonished to have Goon bump violently into him at the corner of the road.

"I just came to meet you," explained Goon in haste. "Thought you mightn't know where the house was. Come on."

He scowled when he saw the five leaning over the gate. He especially scowled at Fatty for deserting him. Gah! Toad of a boy! However, he thought it best to say nothing whatever to any of them, in case Fatty was funny at his expense. Fatty could be rude more politely than any one Goon had ever met.

"I bet Goon's friend will be puzzled to find the house completely empty of kitten, dog, pig, and man," said Fatty. He had brought the kitten with him to Daisy's. It had most conveniently jumped out of the window and landed at his feet while he had been standing laughing at the back of the burgled house. It was now hob-nobbing with Daisy's kitten in a very friendly manner.

P.C. Kenton was indeed astonished to find nothing and no one in the house of the kind that Goon had described.

"Not even Auntie!" he complained. "I was looking forward to seeing Auntie. You sure you weren't Seeing Things, Mr. Goon?"

"I didn't *see* anything – except the kitten. I heard them, I keep telling you," said poor Mr. Goon, amazed to hear no sound of growl or grunt or groan, and to find nothing that could conceivably have made them.

"I can't think where Auntie's gone," said P.C. Kenton, maliciously.

"Don't keep on and on about Auntie," said Mr. Goon, exasperated. "Auntie, whoever she was, wasn't here. The man just kept on wanting her, that's all. I keep telling you."

P.C. Kenton was inclined to make a joke of the whole thing and this infuriated Goon to such an extent that he began to exaggerate.

"If you'd been here and heard a dog growling, just about to leap at you, and heard a pig grunting and stamping about on the floor above, and then heard a man groaning and groaning at the top of his voice, and dragging himself about the floor, well, you wouldn't have made a joke of it, I can tell you," said Mr. Goon.

"Well, all I can say is that the kitten, the pig, the dog, and the man must have all rushed off together as soon as you left the house," said P.C. Kenton, rather severely. "You should have stayed and waited for me. Now we've lost all the animals and the man too. You'll have to make inquiries in the neighbourhood about them. See if any one saw them rushing off together."

Mr. Goon lost some of his high colour. He didn't think people would take him very seriously if he went round asking a question like that. He changed the subject, and after a while the two policemen fastened the open window, and went out of the front door, banging it behind them. The children saw them go.

Mr. Goon crossed to the other side of the road with P.C. Kenton. He didn't want any awkward questions just then, and especially not from Fatty. They passed out of sight.

"A wonderful morning," said Pip, with a sigh. "I've forgotten all about the 'flu'. I wonder doctors don't recommend this sort of thing for 'flu'. I don't see how any one can feel ill if they have mornings like this. I've never laughed so much in my life. What do we do now, Fatty?"

"I want to know if *you've* anything to report to me," said Fatty. "You had the job of going carefully around the house and spotting anything there was to see. Tell me what notes you made?"

"We didn't get much," said Larry. "We've pooled our notes together and here's a short report. I wrote it out while I was waiting for you."

"Good work," said Fatty, approvingly. "Fire ahead." Larry read out his notes.

"We went carefully all round the house. We found out where the burglar came in. He didn't come in at the front door but over the wall at the bottom of the garden."

"How do you know that?" said Fatty, at once.

"Well, there's a bed there, and there are very deep imprints of feet," said Larry. "Only a person jumping down from the wall could have made such deep prints."

"Right," said Fatty. "Go on."

"We traced the same footprints to a bush," went on Larry. "Here the man must have hidden, as there are many footmarks, all messed up together, as if he stood there for some time, occasionally peeping out."

"Got a drawing of the prints?" asked Fatty.

"Of course," said Pip, producing a sheet of paper from his pocket and unfolding it. "But it's not much help – we think the man wore Wellingtons, about size 11. Anyway, the marks are exactly the same as our own Wellington boots make, except that ours are smaller."

"Right," said Fatty again. "Go on."

"We found this cigarette end," said Larry, and passed a damp cigarette butt to Fatty. "Can't tell much from that, though. We could only find this one, and that was under some leaves. I expect Goon found any others there were. We saw what must have been *his* enormous footprints everywhere too. But we know those all right. So we could tell them easily from the others."

"Good thing Goon has such colossal feet," said Fatty. "We always know *his* footmarks! Anything else?"

"Oh yes. We traced the footprints from the bush to the back of the house," said Larry, reading his notes again. "We couldn't see them on the lawn, of course, but we could trace them on another bed and also on a very soggy gravel path by the back of the house. There are quite a lot of marks, all mixed up, on the path under the broken window. He must have got over the wall, hidden under the bush and waited till he judged the time right for entering, then crept up the garden and broken the window. There's a half-brick just below the window. We think he broke it with that."

"Yes, Probably," said Fatty. "That means that some one might have heard him just then. We'll find out. Any more?"

"Yes. There are other footprints, different ones, going from the front door, across the beds there in front of the house, then on a bit of the gravel path that leads to the back gate – then no more," said Larry. "They don't go straight from the front door to the front gate. If they had we wouldn't have seen them, probably, because there are so many other footprints there now."

"I see – so you think some one else – probably Mr. Fellows, say – ran out of the front door, and instead of making straight for the front gate, ran across the front beds to the back gate and disappeared out that way. That probably means he went down the road, not up," said Fatty thoughtfully.

"Yes. That's all our notes," said Larry, shutting his book.

"And jolly good too," said Fatty. "You've done better than old Goon, I bet. Now, just let me think a bit and try to piece out exactly what happened last night."

Is it a Mystery?

"Silence while the Great Mind works," said Larry. "Quiet, Buster! Sh!"

Fatty worked out his ideas rapidly. He was soon ready with them.

"This is how I see it," he said. "Somebody wants something out of Mr. Fellows. What, we don't know. Anyway whatever it is, the man must, for some reason, break into the house – probably because he feels sure that Fellows won't admit him if he comes to the front door. That means that he wants something that Fellows won't want to give him."

"Yes. That sounds right," said Pip. "But why did Fellows tear out of the house like that?"

"Now wait a bit. Don't rush your fences," said Fatty. "The man hides till he thinks it's safe to break in – probably hopes that Fellows is asleep, then he can face him suddenly – possibly with a revolver – and get what he wants. So in he goes at what he thinks is the right moment."

"I'd never have thought of all this," said Bets. "It's like an adventure story, the way you tell it!"

"In he goes," went on Fatty. "But for some reason he doesn't take Fellows by surprise. Perhaps Fellows has heard the breaking of the glass and has smelt a rat – anyway, hearing the man getting in at the back window, what does he do? He shoots out of the front door, leaving it wide open, and rushes out into the dark, dark night...."

"It wouldn't be so very dark," said Daisy. "It was moonlight last night. My bedroom was flooded with it."

"You're right. So was mine. Good for you, Daisy,"

50

said Fatty. "Well, to go on – he fled out into the moon-light night – possibly taking with him whatever it was that the other fellow had come for. The other fellow found the bird flown, but, not being certain if he had taken with him whatever it was he wanted, he proceeded to turn the house upside down to look for it. And my word, he didn't leave any corner or drawer or cupboard – or even the chimneys – unsearched!"

"You *are* clever to work all this out," said Bets. "I never knew any one who could put two and two to-gether and make four so quickly."

"Ah, but where Fatty scores is that he makes them come to *five*," said Larry. "He's always one up on Goon or any one else! Goon makes two and two come to four – but old Fatty goes one better!"

"Thanks, Larry," said Fatty, amused but also pleased. "That's what all good detectives do. Now – the thing is – what was it that Fellows rushed off with? It can't have been anything terribly bulky or heavy or he wouldn't have been able to run far with it – and some one might have spotted him and stopped him if he was carrying a suspicious parcel or big sack."

"So they might," said Daisy. "Gosh, Fatty, if you work all this out much further you'll be telling us what it was the man was carrying."

"I wish I could," said Fatty. "But I think I've found something that might be a help – though how, I can't possibly imagine!"

He produced the little red glove from his pocket. They all stared at it, and Buster sniffed hard.

"It's a doll's glove," said Daisy. "Or a baby's. *Could* it have been a baby's?"

"I did play with the idea that Fellows had kidnapped a baby or some very small child," said Fatty. "But I came to the conclusion he hadn't. There wasn't any-thing in the house to suggest that a small child had been there. Only this glove!"

Larry took the glove and turned it over. "It's very clean," he said. "It couldn't have fitted a child of more than two, I should think. Where's your big doll, Daisy

– the one you had when you were three – it was nearly as big as you then!"

"She's packed away somewhere," said Daisy. "I'll go and get her. Wait a minute."

While she was gone Fatty turned to Pip. "You showed me the drawing of the burglar's footprints," he said. "But what about Fellows' footprints – you saw them from the front door, across the front beds and on the path by the back gate. Did you take a drawing of them?"

"Gosh, yes – I forgot to show it to you," said Pip, feeling in his pocket. He brought out a second folded sheet of paper and undid it carefully. "Rather funny prints these, Fatty – smaller than the others – and rather flat and indistinct."

Fatty looked at them in silence. "I think Fellows ran out in his bedroom slippers," he said. "This print isn't of proper shoes or boots, with heels – it's a print of flat slippers. He may even have had on his night-things and a dressing-gown, with bedroom slippers – he went out in such a hurry. If he was in bed or just going, he wouldn't be fully dressed."

"Yes – you're right. It *is* the print of flat bedroom slippers," said Pip. "Larry, go and get yours – they're flat, aren't they? We could see what kind of footmarks you make in them. There's a nice muddy bit over by the wall."

Larry fetched his slippers and came back with Daisy, who had found the doll. It certainly was a nice big one. Fatty tried the glove on its hand.

"Yes – whatever child this glove belonged to couldn't have been much bigger than your doll, Daisy," he said. "But it beats me why the man dropped it, unless he *was* carrying a small child."

He put the glove back into his pocket and looked at Larry, who was busy changing his Wellingtons for red bedroom slippers.

They all followed him as he went to the muddy path by the wall. "Run over it at top speed," said Fatty. Larry ran, first up, then down.

His mother, looking out of the window just then, was amazed to see Larry rushing up and down in the muddiest part of the garden in his bedroom slippers. She couldn't help noticing them because they were bright red.

She knocked at the window and opened it. "Larry! What are you doing? Stop that silly game at once!'"

"There! We might have known that Mother would look out of the window at this very minute!" said Daisy. "It's all right, Mother – we're just trying to prove something, that's all."

"Well, don't," said her mother. "And please tell the others it's almost one o'clock. I'm sure Pip and Bets ought to be going home."

She shut the window and disappeared. Fatty looked hurriedly but carefully at the flat, smooth prints that Larry's bedroom slippers had made.

"Yes – they're very like Fellows' footprints," he said, comparing them with Pip's drawing. "Do they *look* the same to you, Pip? You got a jolly good view of Fellows' prints because you had to draw them."

"Yes – exactly the same," said Pip. "Come on, Bets, we'll simply have to *tear* home! When's the next meeting, Fatty? Come to our house, will you?"

"Right," said Fatty, folding up the paper and putting it into his pocket. "We'll meet this afternoon at half-past three – unless any one's got to have a rest, because of what the doctor calls 'the aftermath of the 'flu' ' – whatever that means. We've done jolly good work this morning – to say nothing of having had some super fun!"

Larry and Daisy went indoors with the doll and the red bedroom slippers. Pip and Bets shot off home. Fatty went more leisurely, his brain at work. There was more in this little happening than met the eye. Much more, he thought. It wasn't just the ordinary burglary – and Fatty very much doubted if the "burglar" had taken anything at all.

"I bet Mr. Fellows rushed off with whatever it was the man had come after," he thought. "Where is he?

Where did he put what he wanted to hide? Will he come back?"

Mrs. Trotteville was out to lunch, so Fatty was able to have a long and satisfying meal all by himself in front of the fire. He thought about the new problem all the time. It wasn't really a "mystery" – not yet, anyway – but it was certainly very interesting. When Jane the house-parlourmaid came in she was surprised to find how much he had eaten.

"Dear me – yes, I do seem to have cleaned up the dishes rather," said Fatty, gazing in surprise at the empty tureens and meat-dish. "I've been thinking – and when I'm thinking I like plenty of food for thought, Jane. What's the pudding? French pancakes? Oh, good. How many? Ah – plenty of food for thought here!"

Jane laughed. Master Frederick was a caution and no mistake! She went out to tell cook to make another French pancake for Fatty.

Fatty meant to work out a proper scheme for tackling this new problem immediately after lunch – but unfortunately he fell fast asleep in front of the fire, with Buster curled up on the hearth-rug beside him. He didn't wake up till the clock struck half-past three.

He leapt up in horror. Goodness, he ought to be at Pip's by now. He pulled on his coat, remembered his mother's orders to put on a scarf, and took his cap from the peg. He decided to bicycle, with Buster in the front basket. He wouldn't be so late then.

He arrived at Pip's, ringing his bell furiously down the drive, much to Mrs. Hilton's annoyance. Why must Fatty always announce his coming? Really, that boy wanted taking in hand! He was getting too big for his boots.

"Sorry we're late," said Fatty, arriving in the playroom upstairs, with Buster dancing at his heels. "I fell asleep. Can't think why."

"We all did!" said Larry, with a grin. "Another bit of the doctor's 'aftermath', I suppose! Pip and Bets were still asleep when we came!"

"Well, we're wide awake now," said Pip. "And

Mother says you can all stay to tea if you like, Fatty. Our cook has made a big chocolate sponge, so you're lucky. Mother says we can finish it between us, if we like."

"That's one good thing about having had 'flu'," said Bets. "Grown-ups think we want feeding up, and instead of Mother saying 'Now don't be greedy,' she keeps saying, 'You *must* have more than that, dear. Take a second helping, do.' Long may it last!"

Every one agreed heartily. Pip produced the rest of the bull's-eyes that Bets had bought him, and they all took one. They sat round the fire, their cheeks bulging, feeling happy and comfortable.

"Now let's talk," said Larry. "We had to break up the meeting in such a hurry this morning. Fatty, have you any plans? Is this a Mystery, do you think, by any chance? I mean, it seems rather ordinary, really, after the mysteries we've tackled before – but even a *little* one would be nice before we go back to school in four or five days' time."

There were groans at the last few words. Nobody felt like school, but they were all fit enough to go back now.

"I think," said Fatty slowly, "I really do think this *may* be a Mystery, and if so, we'll make the best of it. After all – a Mystery, little or big, is always a Mystery, and has to be solved. I vote we get down to it at once!"

A Few Plans—and a Good Tea

Every one was delighted to hear this, of course. Buster thumped his tail on the floor as if he thoroughly agreed. A Mystery! He'd be in it too, all right!

"You all remember what we worked out this morning, don't you," said Fatty. "And you all know the few clues we have – two sets of footprints – and a small red glove – and a cigarette end that really isn't worth

55

anything as a clue because, except that it proves the intruder smoked, we can't tell much more from it – not even the kind it was."

"Yes. That seems about all the clues," said Larry.

"By the way," said Fatty, remembering something suddenly: "We know how the man got into the garden, hid and then walked to the back window and got in – but does any one know how he got away! I mean – he wasn't in the house the next day – that is, today – so he must have got away somehow. Any ideas?"

"Yes," said Pip at once. "We think he went out of the front door. We thought we could make out a few of his footprints in the general muddle of footmarks going up and down the front path. Anyway there were none going back down the garden."

"I see," said Fatty. "Yes, he probably did go out of the front door – and didn't bang it in case it attracted attention to him. It's a pity we can't find any one who saw either of the men wandering about in the middle of the night – particularly Fellows, who was in bedroom slippers and, presumably, dressing-gown. That's really what we ought to do next – find some one who saw one or other of them that night."

"I don't see how we can," objected Daisy. "We can't possibly find any one who was out late that night and ask them if they saw a man in slippers and dressing-gown. They'd think we were mad."

"Another thing we ought to find out is the time the man entered the house," said Fatty. "That might give us some guide."

"Guide to what?" asked Daisy.

"I don't know," said Fatty. "We've just got to follow up every tiny little thing. Larry, do you know the people next door to you – at the house in between yours and Mr. Fellows?"

"Yes," said Larry. "The mother's help there has a boy. I talk to him sometimes. He's a great bird-fellow – watches them, and knows all their names and calls."

"Is his bedroom on the side next to Mr. Fellows' house?" asked Fatty.

"I don't know," said Larry. "Do you want me to ask him if he heard anything funny in the night – like the breaking of glass, for instance?"

"You might as well," said Fatty. "You see if we can get the time the burglar went in, say at three o'clock in the morning – we could perhaps find some one who saw Fellows somewhere at that time."

"Who?" said Larry thoughtfully. "I mean – how many people are wandering about at three o'clock in the morning?"

"Nobody, usually," said Fatty, mildly, "except Mr. Goon at times. But there are such things as night-watch-men – I don't know if you've ever *heard* of them, Larry – they're the men who . . ."

"All right, all right, you win!" said Larry, making a face. "I should have thought of night-watchmen, of course. Especially as our roads are being done up now, all over the place, and there are night-watchmen to guard the tools and things left beside the road. Yes – you are right – a night-watchman might have spotted Mr. Fellows in his dressing-gown. Though don't forget he might have pulled an overcoat on."

"If it was three o'clock in the morning he would have his pyjamas on, and they would show under an over-coat," said Bets. "It doesn't seem to me to matter whether he wore a dressing-gown or a coat. He'd still look a bit peculiar with pyjama trousers and bedroom slippers!"

"Well, do you propose that we should go round to all the night-watchmen of the district and ask them questions about dressing-gowns and slippers?" said Larry, not at all pleased with the idea. "Bags I don't. Night-watchmen are not awfully helpful in the day time – if you can find them. They're sleepy and cross."

"Well, we'll go when it's dark then," said Fatty. "They will presumably be wide-awake then, if they have a job of watching to do. I think *I'll* go. I don't think the girls should do this – and I doubt if your mothers would let you wander round in the cold night air, Larry and Pip. The aftermath of 'flu' would prevent such goings on!'"

"What about you then?" demanded Pip. "Would you be allowed to?"

"I shall probably feel the need for taking Buster out for a run tonight," said Fatty solemnly. "My father has had to do it while I've been ill, and apparently Buster has played him up properly – run off into the bushes for ages and made Dad hunt for hours – and then he would find Buster waiting patiently for him on the front doorstep."

Every one laughed. "All right – you take old Buster out for a nice long run tonight," said Pip. "And enter into conversation with a few night-watchmen. I can just see you sitting down on an upturned pail and warming your hands at one of those lovely holey buckets of hot cinders, and talking nineteen to the dozen!'"

"And I'll have a word with the boy next door – his name's Erb," said Larry. "Short for Herbert. Or for Erbert, I've never found out which. He's a nice lad, anyway. I'll give you a telephone call, Fatty, if I can find out anything. I'll slip in and see him tonight – lend him a bird-book, or something – and ply him with questions."

"Right – and if as a result of your plying you find out the time of the breaking of the window, it will be a help," said Fatty. "I can ask the night-watchmen if they saw Fellows at some definite time then. It'll make it easier for me."

"How?" asked Bets, puzzled.

"Well – I may have an uncle who sleep-walks and who was missing at a certain time last night, and wants to know where he wandered to, for instance," said Fatty, grinning. "Aha! I'm going to interest quite a few watchmen in my Uncle Horatious."

"I never knew you had an Uncle Horatious," said Bets.

"Didn't you? He's the one that sleep-walks. I've just told you," grinned Fatty. "And I've got an Uncle Tobias who goes round at night seeking for glow-worms

– funny old fellow he is. The night-watchmen might have seen him too."

They all laughed, and Bets gave him a punch. "You're an idiot. You've got an imagination that's too good to be true!"

Buster got up suddenly and ran to the door, standing there with his nose glued to it.

"Buster hears tea coming," said Pip. "I wish I had ears like a dog. By the way, Daisy, how's the little kitten?"

"Fine," said Daisy. "It's a real darling. If it belonged to Mr. Fellows – and I suppose it did – he must be feeling worried about it! I'd hate to desert a tiny thing like that and leave it to starve in an empty house."

"He may come back," said Fatty, "and if he does that'll make a wonderful excuse for going to see him, Daisy! I can take back the kitten, and ask him all sorts of innocent questions!"

"Good idea – *if* he comes back," said Pip. "Hurrah – Buster was right – it *is* the tea!"

He and Bets ran to the door and took in two large and well-loaded trays. "Thanks," said Pip, eyeing the trays with approval. "Gosh – what a wizard chocolate sponge."

It was a very fine tea – hot, new-made scones, sweet and buttery, strawberry jam, bread and butter, and potted salmon and shrimp paste, small ginger buns, shortbread biscuits, and, of course, the large chocolate sponge, which had a thick cream filling.

"I vote we march down in a body to the kitchen after tea and give three cheers," said Larry. "Well, 'flu' certainly has its good points – afterwards! I hope we shall all be fed up just as much in school when we get there."

"We shall be – but not in quite the same way as we are being fed up now!" grinned Pip, offering the scones round. "I soon get fed-up at school."

"Ha ha! Joke over," said Larry, biting into his scone. "Gosh – this is the most buttery scone I ever had. Buster would just love to lick my face clean after it!"

It was a lovely tea – cosy, companionable, and full

of silly jokes. Buster accepted tit-bits from every one, and was not above abstracting a biscuit from the plate when no one was looking.

They ate everything, and Pip asked every one politely if he should go down and ask for any more. But nobody could manage another thing. Buster thumped his tail on the carpet to say that he wouldn't mind a few more biscuits, but unfortunately nobody took any notice of him.

They played a game of Monopoly after tea, but had to stop before it was finished. Both Larry and Daisy had been told to get home by a quarter-past six, as an aunt was coming to stay.

"Will you have time to go in and see that boy next door – Erb, didn't you say his name was?" asked Fatty.

"Oh yes – I'll leave Daisy chatting brightly to Aunt Pamela," said Larry. "She's good at that sort of thing. Well, come on, Daisy. We must go. I'll ring you later on this evening, Fatty."

They all went down to the kitchen and gave three cheers for their good tea. The two maids were tickled and pleased. "Go on with you," said the cook. "You're only doing this to get as good a tea next time you come. Oh, there's Buster. Did they give you any tea, Buster?"

Buster drooped his tail as if to say no. "Oh, you fibber!" said Pip. "Who stole a biscuit off the plate? You thought I wasn't looking, but I was. Good thing I was your host or I'd have had something to say to you!"

Larry, Daisy, and Fatty went to say good-bye and thank you to Mrs. Hilton, who was always very strict about good manners. Then they went off together down the drive to the front gate. Fatty wheeled his bicycle.

"I hope I don't meet Goon," he said. "I've got no lamp at the front. Well, so long, Larry and Daisy. Here's to the new Mystery, even if it's just a tiddler – and don't forget to phone me, Larry."

"Right," said Larry. "And good luck with your Uncle Horatious and your Uncle Tobias and the night-watchmen, Fatty. You'd better keep a sharp eye on those two uncles of yours in future!"

Larry does a Little Work –
and so does Fatty

Larry and Daisy arrived home just at a quarter-past six. Their aunt was already there. Larry chatted politely for ten minutes and then escaped, leaving Daisy to carry on the good work. He slipped up to his room and found his new book on garden birds. Erb would love to borrow that!

He went into the gate of the next-door house and made his way to the back door. He rapped four times. That was the signal to Erb that he had come to see him about something.

Erb opened the door. "Hallo!" he said. "What's up?"

"Nothing," said Larry. "I just wondered if you'd like to borrow my new book. "It's got every single garden bird in it – all the ones we get here, of course!"

"Come in," said Erb, eagerly. "Mum's out. Let's have a look at the book. Coo, it's a beauty! Will you really lend it to me."

Erb sat down at the table and opened the book. He would have been pleased if Larry had gone back home straight away and left him to it. Herbert was certainly mad on birds, Larry reflected.

He wondered how to begin his questions about the night before – when suddenly Erb gave him just the opening he needed.

"Oooh – here's a fine chapter on owls," he said. "And what smashing pictures. I love owls. I'm always listening out for them. There – listen – one's hooting now. Can you hear it?"

A long and beautiful quavering hoot came to Larry's ears. He sat up at once.

"Erb – did you hear any owls last night?"

Erb looked across at Larry and nodded. "Yes, I did. They like moonlight nights, you know. One owl came so near my window that I thought he must be calling for me to come and catch mice with him. I even saw him fly past the window, though I couldn't catch the sound of his quiet wings."

"What time did you hear him?" asked Larry. "Did you notice?"

"Why, did you hear him too?" said Erb, surprised. "Let's see now – I heard owls before I went to sleep – about ten that was. Then they woke me again about half-past twelve – that was the time one came to my window. I got out of bed and watched for a while then."

"Where does your bedroom face – towards our house?" asked Larry.

"No – it faces on to the next-door house," said Erb. "The one that was burgled last night. When I looked out about half-past twelve there was still a light on downstairs in the sitting-room. Mr. Fellows must have been sitting working there like he often does. Sometimes he doesn't draw his curtains, and I see him sitting at a table. But last night the curtains were drawn. He'd got his wireless on, I think. I'm sure I heard sounds coming from it."

"I suppose you didn't hear any owls after that, did you?" asked Larry hopefully. "There must have been a lot about, enjoying looking for mice in the moonlight."

"Oh, there were," said Erb. "Something woke me later on, but I don't think it was owls. I don't really know what it was. I switched on my light and saw it was a quarter-past three. I went to the window and listened for owls again, and I could hear some brown owls somewhere, and some little owls too, twitting like anything."

"Had the light gone out in the sitting-room next door?" asked Larry.

"Oh yes," said Erb. "But the funny thing was that I thought I saw some kind of a light down in the kitchen – the room that faces our kitchen. Not the usual electric light – a torch perhaps, or a candle."

This was all very interesting. Larry wondered if the light in the kitchen had been the torch of the man who had got in through the broken casement.

"Can't you really remember what the sound was, that

woke you?" he asked. "Would it be breaking glass, for instance?"

"Well, it might have been," said Erb, wrinkling his forehead. "Are you thinking about the burglary next door? Well, I dare say that might have been glass breaking I heard, and it might have been the light of a torch I saw in the kitchen, I couldn't swear to it – I didn't take that much notice."

He bent his head down to the book again and became completely absorbed in it. Larry got up. He didn't think he could get anything more out of Erb. Erb obviously took much more interest in birds than he did in burglaries. He didn't seem at all interested in the happenings next door!

"Good-bye, Erb," said Larry, and went back home. Erb and his owls! Larry hoped he would enjoy the bird-book – he deserved the loan of it in return for all the information Larry had got out of him!

He telephoned Fatty and told him the whole conversation clearly and concisely. Fatty approved.

"You are all getting jolly good at reporting things," he said. "Thanks for such interesting details. I think there's no doubt but that the burglar fellow broke the window at about a quarter-past three – and very soon after that Mr. Fellows rushed out of the house probably with the precious goods, whatever they were, that the other chap had come for."

"Well, I suppose you'll now decide that your respected Uncle Horatious wandered abroad sleep-walking at round about a quarter-past three," said Larry, "and half the night-watchmen in Peterswood will hear all about him – bedroom slippers and all!"

"Quite right," said Fatty. "How bright you are, Larry! Anyway, thanks for all you've done. Good work. See you tomorrow and tell you anything that happens tonight!"

That night Fatty apparently went up to bed at eight o'clock, immediately after the evening meal. His mother approved. "You've had a long day and I'm glad you are sensible enough to go up early," she said. "Your father and I are going out to play bridge. Don't read too late in bed, Frederick."

Fatty duly promised, congratulating himself on his luck. He had been afraid that he would have to undress completely and get into bed, in case his mother came up to say good night. Now he needn't do that.

He heard his father get out the car. He heard it go purring down the drive and into the road. Good. Now he could act.

He debated on a disguise. Should he put on one, or shouldn't he? It wasn't really necessary. On the other hand, it would be fun, and he was rather out of practice disguising himself these hols. Fatty decided he *would* do a spot of disguising. He took a torch and he and Buster disappeared cautiously down the garden to the lock-up shed where he kept his dressing-up things.

He thought he wouldn't put on anything too noticeable. He didn't want to scare the night-watchmen, dreaming over their fires! He decided on a small toothbrush moustache, his false, prominent teeth, and no wig – just his own hair. A cap of some sort? Yes, that check one would do well. He'd wear it back to front – it would look very fetching that way.

He chose a tweed overcoat, rather too big for him, and a blue-spotted scarf. He looked at himself in the glass. Did he look like a young man asking for information about a sleep-walking uncle? He thought he did.

He set off. He guessed he must go in the direction of the river, because Mr. Fellows had gone out of the back gate, which meant he was presumably going in that direction and not up the road towards the hills. Now, where was the road being mended on the way to the river?

Fatty decided regretfully to leave Buster behind. Too many people knew Buster. If they met him in company with a strange young man at night, they might think somebody was stealing him. So Buster was left behind, curled up on the rug in the shed.

Fatty went to Mr. Fellows' house, and looked at it. It was in complete darkness. He stood at the back gate

Fatty and Buster crept cautiously down the garden

and looked along the road. Yes – he would go down there – and when he came to the bottom he would see if there was any sign of a night-watchman's brazier of glowing coals.

He walked down smartly. At the end he looked this way and that. No sign of any watchman or of the road being up. He turned to the right and made his way to the next cross-road. There he had some luck.

Red lamps burned in a row, and in the midst of them was the dark shadowy shape of a watchman's hut, with the brazier of burning coals in front of it. Fatty walked along.

The watchman heard his steps and peered out. "Good evening," said Fatty cheerily. "Nice fire you've got there! Do you charge anything if I warm my hands, mate?"

"Warm 'em and welcome," said the old fellow, sucking at a pipe. "Everybody who comes by likes a warm at my fire, so he do."

"Do you get many people late at night?" asked Fatty, spreading his fingers over the warm glow. "I mean, after midnight?"

"I get the policeman, Mr. Goon," said the watchman. "Chatty fellow he is. Handles a lot of important cases, so he tells me. And I gets a fisherman or two, that likes a bit of midnight fishing. Nobody about then to disturb the fish you know."

"I wonder if you've ever seen my Uncle Horatious," began Fatty. "He's a funny old fellow – walks in his sleep."

"Do he now?" said the watchman, with interest.

"Yes, he do – er, does," said Fatty. "I suppose you didn't see him last night, did you, wandering about in a dressing-gown – or perhaps a coat over his pyjamas – with bedroom slippers on his feet?"

The watchman went off into a cackle of laughter just like a goose. Fatty listened to it intently – he could copy that at some time – wonderful! Cackle, cackle, cackle.

"Naw, I didn't see him," said the old man. "Good thing too, or mebbe I'd have thought I were asleep, and dreaming – and that's not a good thing for a night-watchman to do. But old Willie, him that's watching farther along, nearer the river, he did say something about a chap in pyjamas last night. Mebbe that was your Uncle Horatious. You should ought to lock him up, Mister – he'll get himself drownded one night, sleep-walking near the river!"

"Yes. I think I *will* lock him up in the future," said Fatty, delighted at this unexpected bit of news. "I'll go and have a word with Willie. Hallo – who's this?"

There was a ringing of a bicycle bell, and a familiar figure loomed up in the light of the nearest lamp-post. Goon! Blow! What was *he* doing here?

A Little Night-Prowling

Fatty moved off hastily, glad that he hadn't brought Buster with him. What a welcome Buster would have given the astonished Goon!

The burly policeman got off his bicycle and went over to the night-watchman. Fatty escaped into the shadows and hurried off to find Willie.

A row of red lamps again guided him. He went down a long road towards them, seeing the flash of the river at the end. The watchman's little hut was set close beside the bright brazier of burning coals.

Fatty introduced himself as before, and brought his Uncle Horatious into the conversation as soon as he could. He was afraid that Goon might turn up again! Why must he ride round the streets just when Fatty wanted them to himself!

Willie the watchman proved rather a surly fellow. He answered very shortly indeed.

"You sometimes have people asking you if they can warm themselves by your fine fire, I'm sure," said Fatty, persevering in spite of the watchman's surliness. "I bet my Uncle Horatious always comes to warm himself when he goes sleep-walking at nights."

The watchman grunted. He took no interest in Fatty's uncle or in sleep-walking either.

"You might have seen the old chap last night," went on Fatty. "Came out in his pyjamas and bedroom slippers. Ha, ha, ha!"

The watchman looked at Fatty. "I seed him," he remarked, suddenly developing quite a chatty manner. "Leastways, I seed some one running by – pyjama legs and bedroom slippers 'e wore. Scatty fellow, I thought to myself. But he weren't old, the way he run along."

Fatty was delighted. Ah – so Mr. Fellows had run down this road. That was something! It only led to the river. Why had he gone down to the *river*?

"Was he carrying anything?" asked Fatty.

"Yes, he were. Something in his arms, like, but I dunno what it was," said the watchman. "So he were your uncle, were he? Do he often sleep-walk?"

"On moonlight nights mostly," said Fatty, ready to invent anything, now that he had got a little information. "You didn't see him come back, did you?"

"Naw," said Willie, and relapsed into surliness again. Fatty was about to say good night when he heard the ringing of a bicycle bell again. Surely, surely that couldn't be Goon once more?

But it was! Fatty escaped from the light of the burning brazier just in time. Goon sailed up to the light of the red lamps and hailed Willie.

"Are you there, my man? I want to ask you a few questions!"

Fatty hid behind a convenient bush, a really worrying suspicion forming in his mind. Was Goon cross-examining the night-watchman too – and for the same reason as Fatty was? Had he worked out the problem in the same way as the Find-Outers had? If so, Goon was growing a few brains!

"Well, Willie," said Goon, warming himself at the brazier, first his vast front, then his rather vaster back.

"You seen any one suspicious last night? I'm on a case again, and I'm looking out for some one."

"You wouldn't be wanting an old Uncle what sleep-walks and wears pyjamas and red slippers, would you?" said Willie.

Goon stared at him, astonished. "Why, the old watch-man away up the other road asked me that," he said. "I thought it was just his joke. Who's been kidding you along too?"

"A young fellow," said Willie. "Proper worried about his old uncle Horatious, he was – old gent what sleep-walks at night."

"Oh. And I suppose Uncle Horatious went for a sleep-walk last night, did he?" said Mr. Goon, in such a ferocious voice that Willie was astonished.

" 'Ere! What you talking to me like that for?" he complained.

"What was this fellow like who told you this fairy-tale?" demanded Mr. Goon.

"I didn't rightly notice him much," said Willie. "My eyes ain't too good now. Young, he was. Tallish. A moustache of some sort. And he was fattish too."

Mr. Goon gave an exclamation. *Fattish!* Could the owner of the sleep-walking uncle be – that fat boy! Was it that pest again, On the Track of Something as usual? Mr. Goon could have shouted in rage.

The moustache was put on, of course – the sleep-walking uncle was made up. It must be – it *was* that fat boy following the same clues as he, Mr. Goon, had so painfully worked out himself. Where was he? Where had he gone? If Mr. Goon could have got his hands on Fatty at that moment, Fatty would have had to yell for mercy!

"Now, you listen here, Willie," said Mr. Goon, sud-denly making a plan. "You listening?"

"Ay," said Willie. "Speak louder, though. My ears ain't so good."

Mr. Goon spoke up, much to Fatty's joy. What was he going to say?

"That fellow will come back this way," said Mr.

69

Goon. "I want to get my hands on him, see? So when you see him coming, you holler out to him. Get him over here and keep him talking."

"What for?" asked Willie, doubtfully. "If he's a bad lot I don't want to give 'im the chance of knocking me on the 'ead."

"I'm going to hide at the other end of the road," said Goon. "In case he spots me. He's scared of me, dead scared. If he so much as sees the lamp on my bike he'll run for miles. And I want to get my hands on him, see? Now, when you see him coming, you take up one of your red lamps and swing it slowly to and fro in your hands. I'll be along at once, while you're talking to him."

"All right," said Willie, resignedly. What with people talking about sleep-walking uncles and red slippers and bad lots and swinging lamps, Willie was fed up. He'd never get down to a nice little snooze tonight, that was certain!

Mr. Goon disappeared on his bicycle. He went to the far end of the river road, got off, and hid under a tree, his bicycle beside him. Ah – he'd catch that fat boy on his way back! He'd have to come back that way, because the river barred his way at the other end of the road!

Fatty debated what to do. Should he cut down to the river, make his way across somebody's back garden, and cut into the road that ran parallel with this? Or should he play a little trick on Goon?

He decided on the trick. Goon deserved one after saying that Fatty was dead scared of him! Fatty began to get to work quickly. He blackened his face with dirt. He twisted his cap the other way round, with the peak now shading his eyes. He put a white handkerchief round his neck instead of the scarf. He took off his moustache, but left in his awful teeth.

He felt about on the waste piece of ground nearby. Was there anything he could use in his trick. His hand fell upon an old sack. Good – just the thing! Fatty groped about among the rubbish left by the road-menders and came across pieces of brick and stone. He quickly slid them into the sack until it was half full. It was very heavy.

He made his way back to the road and skirted round to the back of the watchman. Then he walked slowly by him, half bent under the sack.

The watchman saw him, but his bleary old eyes couldn't make out who it was. He stared hard, in doubt, wishing the moon would come out from behind a cloud. He decided that whoever it was looked decidedly suspicious. It wouldn't do any harm to swing the red lamp to and fro!

He picked it up, turned himself towards Mr. Goon, and swung the lamp slowly. Fatty grinned as he saw it out of the corner of his eye. He plodded on slowly, bent under the sack. If ever any one looked a suspicious person at that moment, Fatty did!

Mr. Goon saw the swinging lamp, and came quickly down the road, keeping to the shadows, his rubber-soled boots making no noise. He tried to see if Fatty was there, talking to the watchman. But, to his great annoyance, when he got to the little hut there was no one there but Willie!

"Where is he? Why did you swing your lamp? He's not here!" said Goon, exasperated.

"I see a very suspicious chap shuffling down the river road," said Willie. "Not the chap as you wanted – but some one you'd like to get your hands on, I don't doubt. A real suspicious chap. And carrying a heavy sack too. You'd like to know what's in that sack, I reckon!"

"Ho! It certainly sounds bad," said Goon, thinking that if he couldn't get his hands on Fatty, it would be satisfactory to get them on to some one else. "What direction did he go in?"

"Yonder," said Willie, nodding. And yonder went Goon, keeping to the shadows, tracking down Fatty and the suspicious sack. Fatty took a quick look back. Good! Goon was on his trail! He would lead him a nice little dance!

Down to the river plodded Fatty, and came to where

the waves were silvery with moonlight. He turned down the towing-path that led to the small jetty nearby. Goon followed stealthily, breathing so hard that Fatty could hear him.

Fatty walked slowly shuffling one foot after the other, like an old, old man. He coughed mournfully as he went, a horrible hollow cough. He suddenly stopped and put down his sack as if it was too heavy. Goon stopped too.

Fatty heaved the sack on to his shoulder again, and set off once more on his way to the jetty. He stopped suddenly again when he was almost there and put the sack down once more, with a groan. Goon also stopped suddenly. He was very curious now. What was the old man doing with such a heavy sack? Where was he going? What was in the sack? Had he some accomplice he was meeting? Goon began to feel excited.

Fatty hoisted the sack on his back once again and went on his way. He came to the little wooden jetty. Moonlit water splashed against it. Fatty went on to the jetty and sat down with his sack as if to rest.

Now was Goon's chance! He emerged from the shadows and strode heavily up to the jetty, a big figure in the moonlight.

"Now then," he began. "What's your name? And what have you got in that sack?"

"Bricks and stones," said Fatty, truthfully, in a sad, weary, old-man voice.

"Gah!" said Goon, in scorn. "Nobody carries sacks of bricks and stones about, unless they're mad!"

"Mebbe I'm mad," said Fatty, drooping his head down so that the moonlight didn't fall on his face.

"You open that sack and let me see what you've got," said Goon, threateningly.

"No," said Fatty, clutching the sack as if it contained rubies and diamonds.

"Come on, now!" said Goon, advancing on him. "You open that sack – and be quick about it!"

72

"It don't belong to me," said Fatty, obstinately, still clutching the sack.

"Who does it belong to then?" demanded Mr. Goon.

"Sh! It belongs to Mr. Fellows!" whispered Fatty, on the spur of the moment, and then was horrified to realize what he had said! Mr. Goon was amazed.

"Belongs to Mr. Fellows!" he repeated. "But – how did you get it? Look here, you give it to me. You are acting in a suspicious manner, and you'll be arrested in a moment!"

He grabbed at the sack, and Fatty stood up, shouting dramatically, "No, no, don't touch it!" And then, more dramatically, he picked up the sack and flung it down into the river beside the jetty. He was very glad to get rid of it indeed. It made a most tremendous splash.

Mr. Goon was bitterly disappointed. He had made up his mind that there was something very important in the sack – and now it was gone! He knelt down to look over the side of the jetty – and Fatty took to his heels at once.

Mr. Goon stood up and gaped at the running figure. How could the old, shuffling fellow run like that? Mr. Goon wondered if he was dreaming. He decided that he couldn't possibly catch the fellow – why, he was almost at the turning into the river-road now! What a strange thing to run like that after so much shuffling! A sentence floated into Mr. Goon's mind – "Fear lent him wings". Well, Mr. Goon hadn't got any wings. He would have to walk back at his own pace.

He knelt down again to look into the river, but, of course, he could see no sign of the sack. He made up his mind to come with a boat-hook the next day and haul it up. He would find out what was in that sack if he had to go into the water himself to get it!

Willie was astonished to see yet another figure, this

time racing past, instead of shuffling past. The goings-on there were in these times! It was quite certain he wouldn't get a snooze before midnight at this rate. That policeman would probably be coming back in a minute too.

Fatty fell to a walk after a bit. He guessed Mr. Goon wouldn't come after him. He felt relieved to think that the policeman hadn't recognized him. But whatever had made him say the sack belonged to Mr. Fellows? That was really rather idiotic, and not fair to Mr. Fellows! Fatty felt distinctly uncomfortable about that.

He got home without any further adventure, feeling unexpectedly tired. Buster gave him an uproarious welcome, and Fatty discarded all his clothes down in the old shed with the little Scottie dancing round him in delight.

Then Fatty crawled tiredly up the garden path from the shed to the house. "Gosh! I'm shuffling just like I pretended to," he marvelled. "But shuffling's not so good when it's real!"

Fatty was so tired that he was almost asleep as he climbed the stairs. He fell into bed, and immediately began to dream of red lamps following him in a threatening manner. He groaned in his sleep and Buster pricked up one ear. Then Mr. Goon appeared in his dream riding on his bicycle – and fortunately the red lamps all attached themselves to him, so Fatty was at peace once more.

At breakfast the next morning the telephone rang. The maid came in and looked at Fatty. "It's for you, Master Frederick," she said. "Master Larry on the phone."

Fatty jumped up as if dogs were after him. There must be Something Up if Larry telephoned so early! He hurried to the telephone.

"That you, Fatty?" came Larry's excited voice. "I say – Mr. Fellows is back! I thought you'd better know at once in case old Goon doesn't know yet."

"Gosh, yes – thanks for phoning," said Fatty. "But how did you know?"

"Erb told me," said Larry. "I was out in the garden

74

with Daisy looking for one of the kittens that wouldn't come in, and Erb called over the wall to me. He said he was awake last night, listening to his precious owls again, when he heard the click of the gate next door."

"Go on," said Fatty. "What time was this?"

"He said it was about two o'clock in the morning," said Larry. "He went to his window at once, wondering if it was a burglar again – but he says it was Mr. Fellows. He saw him clearly in the moonlight. And he saw him again when he went into the house, because he switched the light on in the sitting-room whose window Erb can see into. And it *was* Mr. Fellows all right."

"What was he dressed in?" asked Fatty, excited by this news.

"He couldn't really see – but he *thinks* he had on a dressing-gown," said Larry. "He wasn't carrying anything though – so if he did rush out of the house with a parcel of some sort . . ."

"He did!" said Fatty. "I found that out from a night-watchman last night!"

"Oh, good – well, whatever it was, he apparently didn't bring it back with him," said Larry. "Do you suppose he was shocked to see his house turned upside down?"

"No. He probably expected it," said Fatty. "Well – I'll be along at your house after breakfast. Telephone Pip and Bets, will you? We'll have to think out our next move. By the way, Goon's on the same track as we are. He was very chatty with the watchmen last night too – seems to me as if he's been setting his brains to work. Most unusual!"

"Frederick!" called his mother. "Your breakfast is getting cold. Do come back."

"Good-bye – see you later, Larry," said Fatty hastily, wondering just how much of the telephone conversation his mother had heard.

He went back into the dining-room and sat down. "That was Larry," he said. "We're all going to his house this morning, if that's all right, Mother. You don't want me for anything, do you?"

75

"Well, I *was* going to look through all your school clothes," said his mother. "But it will do another time."

Fatty groaned. "School! I'm usually jolly pleased to go back – but this 'flu' has taken it out of me. I'd like the hols to be longer this time!"

"You look the picture of health," said his father, putting his newspaper down. "And judging by the number of sausages you've eaten you feel healthy enough too. You'll go back to school on the right day, so don't try to get round your mother."

"I'm not!" said Fatty indignantly. "And sausages have nothing to do with how I feel. Actually, I was eating them quite absent-mindedly this morning."

"What a waste of sausages then," said his father, putting up his newspaper again. "Frederick, I couldn't help overhearing part of your telephone conversation just now – I hope you are not going to get mixed up in anything to do with that absurd policeman again."

"Not if I can help it," said Fatty, spreading butter on his toast. "Any news in the paper this morning, Dad?"

"Plenty. And I'm quite aware that you are hurriedly changing the subject," said Mr. Trotteville, drily.

Fatty said no more, but chewed his toast, his mind dwelling on the return of Mr. Fellows. He would go and see him immediately after breakfast, taking the kitten with him – what a marvellous excuse for going! He would see what he could get out of him. He hoped that Mr. Goon didn't also know Mr. Fellows was back, but there was really no reason why he should have heard. Erb wouldn't have told *him*!

"Good old Erb!" thought Fatty, drinking his coffee. Erb had come in very useful indeed. Good thing he was so interested in night-birds! He wouldn't have been nearly so useful if his interest had been in house sparrows.

Fatty took his bicycle and rode off to Larry's at top speed, with Buster in the basket. On the way he saw Mr. Goon, also on a bicycle, far in the distance. The policeman saw Fatty and waved to him frantically. He had a few questions to ask him about the night before!

76

Fatty knew that. He certainly wasn't going to stop! He waved back cheerily, as if he thought that Goon was simply being friendly. The policeman pedalled furiously to catch up with Fatty.

"Blow him," thought Fatty, and pedalled as fast as he could. He turned a corner, leapt off his bicycle and disappeared with it into the garden of an empty house. He crouched behind the fence.

Mr. Goon came by, purple and panting, and sailed up the road, marvelling that Fatty could disappear so swiftly. Fatty came out quickly, mounted his bicycle and rode off in the opposite direction. Buster was surprised at all this, but hadn't even got out of the basket!

"Goon's on the lookout for me," thought Fatty. "I'll have some awkward questions to answer. Blow him! Does he suspect it was me last night that he followed? I wonder if he's found that sack of bricks and stones yet! He said he was going to get a boat-hook and drag it up. Well, good luck to him! It'll keep him out of the way for a bit, messing about in the river!"

He arrived at Larry's out of breath. Pip, Bets, Larry, and Daisy were watching for him. Daisy was holding the kitten.

"Nobody's seen a sign of Mr. Fellows," said Larry, as soon as Fatty came up. "We think he may be lying low for a bit. Do you think you really should go and see him? I mean – he mayn't be at all pleased to see you!"

"Can't help that," said Fatty. "I can't miss this chance. I simply must question him before Goon gets at him."

He took the kitten. "Thanks, Daisy. Well, you funny little thing? You won't like leaving your playmate, will you, and going back to that lonely house!"

He left his bicycle at Larry's, and went up the road to the next house but one – Mr. Fellows'. He looked in at the gate. Should he go to the front door or to the back? There was no sign of life in the place at all. Was Mr. Fellows pretending to be still away?

"I'll go round to the back," thought Fatty. "I don't want Goon to see me standing at the front door if he comes by."

He went quietly and cautiously round to the back. He looked in at the window there, the one that was broken. Nobody was about. Fatty debated with himself again.

It was likely that Mr. Fellows would not answer any ringing or knocking if he was lying low. But *some*how Fatty must get hold of him. How? Fatty racked his brains.

And then a splendid idea came to him. It was quite likely that Mr. Fellows had been looking for the kitten, now he was back – perhaps he was worried about it. Fatty would stick his face close to the broken pane, and miaow as loudly as he could! If that didn't fetch Mr. Fellows into the kitchen, nothing would!

An Interesting Conversation

"Miaow! Miaow! MIAOW!"

A most pitiful, heart-rending noise penetrated into the kitchen through the broken window. The little kitten that Fatty was holding jumped when it heard his life-like mewing. It suddenly added its own high-pitched mew.

"That's right," whispered Fatty. "Keep up the good work, kitty. Mew as loudly as you can!"

"Miaow!" said the kitten obligingly. "Miaow."

Fatty listened. He thought he heard a noise in the house. It seemed to come from upstairs.

"MIAOW-ee-ow-ee-OW!" said Fatty piercingly.

He listened again. Yes, certainly some one was moving in the house now – there were footsteps on the stairs. Then they stopped.

"Miaow," said the kitten shrilly. It certainly was doing its best for Fatty.

A man appeared at the inner door of the kitchen, the one that led into the hall.

"That must be Fellows," thought Fatty, looking at him closely. He was fully dressed, though Fatty had half expected him to be in dressing-gown and slippers!

He hadn't caught sight of the boy and the kitten yet. He was looking all round the kitchen floor as if wondering where the mewing had come from. He was a young-ish fellow, with a thin face, and bright, intelligent eyes. His hair was smoothly brushed, and he didn't in the least look as if he had rushed panic-stricken out of his house two nights before.

"Miaow," said the kitten again, struggling to get out of Fatty's arms. The man heard the mew and looked across to the window. He saw Fatty's head and shoulders there, and made as if to draw back at once. Then he saw that Fatty was a boy, and that he was holding the kitten.

He came forward slowly. Fatty guessed that he was annoyed at having been seen. He spoke apologetically through the broken pane.

"Sorry to disturb you, sir – but this is your kitten, isn't it? We've been looking after it through the – er – upset."

The man smoothed back his hair. He answered cautiously. "Yes – it's my kitten. Er – wait a minute, I'll undo the kitchen door."

He unlocked and unbolted it. Fatty was at the door, waiting. The man stretched out his hand for the kitten, and Fatty sensed that once he had taken it, he would probably say no more than a word of thanks, and shut the door.

"I say, sir – your burglary caused quite an excitement!" said Fatty, holding on to the kitten. "The police were here – did you know?"

Mr. Fellows looked startled. "The police!" he said. "What for? How did they know anything about the house being empty – or, er – burgled?"

Fatty thought rapidly. Mr. Fellows hadn't heard then that the milkman had reported anything – he didn't know that Mr. Goon had inspected the house and found it upside down. Probably he hoped that nobody knew anything at all, either about the intruder, or about his rushing out of the house!

"I'll tell you all about it, if you like, sir," said Fatty,

79

stepping firmly into the kitchen. Mr. Fellows now obviously wanted to know what Fatty had to say. It was news to him that the police had been into his house. He looked worried.

He shut the kitchen door and locked it. He took Fatty into the little sitting-room. Everything was now tidy and in its place. Mr. Fellows had obviously been very busy since he had got back, and had cleared everything up. The kitten followed, mewing.

"Does it want any milk?" asked Mr. Fellows, looking down at it. "I'm afraid there isn't any. The milkman apparently didn't come this morning."

"No. I expect the police told him not to as you weren't here," said Fatty. He sat down on a chair.

"What *is* all this about the police!" said Mr. Fellows irritably. "Can't a man go away for a short while without the police coming in and snooping round! I think that is most unnecessary."

"Well, you see, apparently burglars got in and turned the place upside down while you were away," said Fatty, watching Mr. Fellows closely. "Didn't you find everywhere in an awful mess?"

The man hesitated. He quite obviously wasn't going to say more than he needed to.

"Yes – but I'm an untidy person," he said. "Er – who did you say gave the alarm to the police?"

"The milkman," said Fatty, stroking the purring kitten. "He found the front door wide open when he came to leave your milk yesterday morning – walked in, saw the confusion, and telephoned the police."

"I see," said Mr. Fellows. "This is all news to me."

"What time did you leave your house then?" asked Fatty suddenly. He knew quite well what time it had been, because of Erb's information, but he wanted to see what Mr. Fellows had to say.

The man hesitated again. "Oh, sometime that night," he said. "I – er – went to visit a friend and stayed the night with him. I came back last night – to find the house a little untidy, certainly. But nothing has been
80

stolen as far as I can see. I don't see why the police had to butt in without my permission."

"Because of the open front door," said Fatty, patiently. "I suppose you did shut the front door after you when you went out, Mr. Fellows?"

"Of course," said the man, but Fatty didn't believe him. He felt sure that Mr. Fellows had probably only pulled it to, not wanting the intruder in the house to hear him go. It was the intruder who had left it wide open!

Fatty debated whether or not to ask Mr. Fellows what he had been dressed in when he had left the house. He decided that he wouldn't. He would only be more on his guard than ever, and would anyhow lie about it. Fatty glanced at him – he looked extremely clean and tidy and well brushed.

"Not a bit like my Uncle Horatious!" thought Fatty. "Now – if I want to find out if he really did wander about in a dressing-gown and bedroom slippers, I'll somehow have to slip upstairs and snoop round for them. But how?"

All conversation suddenly came to an abrupt end. A big red face unexpectedly appeared at the sitting-room window, and looked in. The face owned a helmet – it was Goon!

Mr. Fellows gave an exclamation. "Who's that? Of all the brazen cheek! It's the police again! What do they think they're doing, snooping and prying on private property like this? I'll put this fellow where he belongs!"

"I certainly would, if I were you," Fatty agreed fervently. "A man can't call his house his own these days! Are you going to let that policeman in, sir? He's speaking to you."

Goon had just been on his rounds, and had, as a matter of routine, called in at Mr. Fellows' house to see if anything had happened there. As there was no smoke from the chimneys, and everything seemed quiet, he hadn't done anything but peep in at the windows. He wasn't going to enter that house alone again if he could help it!

He could hardly believe his eyes when he saw Fatty

sitting there with a man who must be Fellows. He gaped at them both. Then a familiar rage boiled up in him. That boy! That toad! There he was again, poking his nose in – and getting it there before he, Mr. Goon, could get in his. How did he do it?"

"Open the door, sir," bellowed Mr. Goon. "I have a few words to say to you."

Mr. Fellows glared at the red-faced policeman. He strode to the window and opened it.

"What do you mean by peering in like this at my window?" Mr. Fellows asked in a furious voice. "Can't you see I'm sitting here talking to a friend? What's the matter with you?"

"A friend?" choked Mr. Goon, glaring at Fatty. "Is that boy your friend?"

"I shall report you for this extraordinary behaviour," said Mr. Fellows. "My house is my own, and I am not aware that I have done anything to cause the police to pry into it."

"But – but – there's been a burglary!" spluttered Mr. Goon. "The house was all upside down, and . . ."

"There has been no burglary," said Mr. Fellows. "As far as I know not a single thing has been stolen. As for the house being untidy, well, I'm an untidy person. I can turn my own house upside down if I want to, can't I?"

"The front door was wide open," persisted Mr. Goon, angry and bewildered.

"I'm forgetful," said Mr. Fellows. "I do sometimes forget to close my doors. Now – clear off – do you hear me, CLEAR OFF!"

Fatty could have hugged himself in joy. Goon was always yelling at people to clear off – and now here was some one yelling the same thing at him. But the policeman had not finished yet.

"Well, let me tell you you've no right to go away and leave animals to starve in the house," he said.

"The kitten is quite all right," said Mr. Fellows coldly, and was about to shut the window when Mr. Goon put an enormous dark-blue arm in to stop him.

"What about the dog?" he said. "And the pig?"

Mr. Fellows stared at Mr. Goon as if he had suddenly taken leave of his senses. "What dog and what pig?" he demanded. "Are you crazy, constable?"

"Ho! And what about the fellow who kept crying out, and wanted his auntie?" said Mr. Goon, trying to force the window open

Mr. Fellows was now quite convinced that Mr. Goon was raving mad. He turned to speak to Fatty – but Fatty was not there!

No – Fatty had seen a chance to creep upstairs and examine bedroom slippers and dressing-gowns, and also pyjamas. Reluctant as he was to leave the battleground on which Mr. Fellows and Mr. Goon were squabbling so fiercely, he felt that he couldn't miss this chance.

He picked up the kitten and tiptoed out of the room. He wanted the kitten with him to provide him with an excuse for going upstairs – why should any one think it odd if the kitten fled upstairs and needed looking for?

Up the stairs went Fatty, grinning to hear Mr. Goon shouting the questions about the dog and the pig. Gosh, Mr. Fellows would think he was quite mad!

He saw that everywhere had been tidied up. He tiptoed into the biggest room, which he guessed was Mr. Fellows' bedroom. Now – where were his slippers – and pyjamas – and dressing-gown?

Fatty is Pleased

Fatty looked round the room. No slippers to be seen! He looked under the bed. Ah – a pair of red slippers lay there, rather like Larry's, but bigger. Fatty turned them upside down and examined them.

They were muddy, very muddy! Mud had even got splashed on the tops of the slippers. It was quite obvious that Mr. Fellows had been wandering about the streets in these.

Fatty slipped his hand under the eiderdown and

pulled out pyjamas, striped red and white. He gave a low whistle. The bottom edges of the legs were filthy dirty – splashed with mud and clay. Fatty nodded his head. Yes – that muddy clay down by the river.

Now for the dressing-gown. It was hanging in a tall cupboard. It was dirty – but it was also messed up with hay and straw – strands stuck out here and there. Where had Mr. Fellows been in his dressing-gown? Fatty thought rapidly, as he shut the cupboard door.

"He didn't go to stay with a friend, he hid somewhere for the rest of that night, and all day yesterday – because he didn't want to be found in his night-clothes – questions would be asked! He hid in a barn or in a hay-stack or rick – and crept home in the middle of last night. I bet the watchmen were surprised to see him again, if they spotted him. Gosh, they'd think my Uncle Horatious had been out again!"

The angry voices downstairs had stopped. There was the sound of a window being slammed shut. Fatty dropped down on his hands and knees and began calling.

"Puss, puss, where are you? Kitty, kitty!"

A voice came up the stairs. "What are you doing up there? Come down at once!"

"Sorry," said Fatty, appearing at the top of the stairs. "The kitten's run away."

"It's down here," said Mr. Fellows. He still looked very angry. "You clear off now. Thanks for seeing to the kitten. I've ticked that interfering policeman off, and he's gone. I've a good mind to report him."

"I should, sir," said Fatty earnestly.

"I think he must be mad," said Mr. Fellows, lighting a cigarette and pacing nervously up and down. "Talking about dogs and pigs and aunties."

Fatty wanted to laugh. He glanced round, and decided that there really wasn't any more to get out of Mr. Fellows, or to hunt for in the house. He had done very nicely!

"Well, good-bye, sir – and I hope the kitten will be all right now," said Fatty. "Sorry to intrude and all that. Fancy you not having a burglar in after all!"

"Well, I didn't," snapped Mr. Fellows. "Clear out now. I want some peace!"

Fatty cleared out, whistling softly. A most interesting interview – and how nice to find that all his ideas had been right. Those muddy slippers! My word, if Goon once got into the house and did a bit of snooping he would find a few things to interest him too!

Mr. Goon was lying in wait for Fatty. He emerged from behind a tree as Fatty turned down the road to go to Larry's.

"Ho!" said Mr. Goon, his face purple. "Ho!" He seemed quite unable to say anything else for the moment.

"Ho to you," said Fatty politely. "Many Hoes!"

Mr. Goon went a deeper purple. "So you're his friend, are you?" he said, in a choking voice. "*That's* a bit of news, that is!"

"I'm so glad," said Fatty, politely, trying to edge past.

"Do you know what you are?" said Mr. Goon, losing the rest of his temper with a rush. "You're a Pest! A Toad! But I've sent in my report, see – and you'll be sorry!"

"I don't see why," said Fatty. "I do hope you've put in the kitten, the dog, and the pig – not forgetting Auntie."

"There wasn't any Auntie," shouted Mr. Goon. "He just *wanted* his Auntie! Gah! What with you and Kenton and that fellow up yonder, my life's not worth living."

"No. It's a poor sort of life," agreed Fatty, suddenly seeing Larry and Daisy out of the corner of his eye in Larry's front garden. He hoped and prayed they had got Buster with them, and would have the sense to let him out of the gate.

"I suppose you think I don't know it was you muddling those night-watchmen last night?" began Goon again, going off on a new track, with a new grievance. "Your Uncle Horace! Pah!"

"My Uncle *Horatious*," corrected Fatty. "Don't muddle up my uncles, please."

Mr. Goon advanced on him, ready to tear Fatty limb

from limb. Never had he felt so angry in his life. Poor Mr. Goon – he was muddled and bewildered and so exasperated that he didn't know which way to turn!

"Wuff! Wuff-Wuff!"

With a delighted volley of barks, Buster suddenly shot out of Larry's front gate at sixty miles an hour. He was thrilled to see Fatty, and equally thrilled to see Mr. Goon, though for rather a different reason. He leapt up at Fatty, gave him a hurried lick, and then leapt at Mr. Goon.

The policeman was defeated. Fatty was bad enough – but Fatty plus Buster was too much. Mr. Goon gave the biggest snort of his life, flung himself on his bicycle and wobbled down the hill, one of his feet slipping frantically on a pedal. Buster flew after him, leaping and pouncing in delight.

Fatty began to laugh. He staggered into Larry's gate. Larry held him up, laughing too. The other three were there and they made their way to the out-house at the bottom of the garden. Fatty collapsed on the ground, quite weak with excitement and laughter.

They held a very interesting meeting. Every one hung on Fatty's words as he described his peculiar interview with Mr. Fellows, Goon's sudden appearance, and all that Fatty had discovered in his snooping upstairs.

"I say! Then all your reasoning was correct," said Bets, in admiration. "Every single thing! He did rush out in pyjamas and dressing-gown and slippers – and he came back in them too – after sleeping in hiding somewhere."

"Yes. But we still don't know what he took with him when he went – or where he has hidden it," said Fatty. "According to Erb he had nothing with him when he returned. He wouldn't, anyway, I suppose – because it would be senseless to take back whatever it was that was so valuable. He might find the burglar waiting for him again!"

"Yes. He's hidden it," said Larry. "I wonder where. We can't very well hunt in all the haystacks and ricks round about Peterswood – there are dozens of them!"

"He's very careful in all he says," said Fatty. "There's

86

something going on. I wonder what it is. Gosh, we *must* try and find out before we go back to school. An unfinished Mystery. How disgraceful!"

Every one agreed, but nobody could see for the life of them how they could get any further. Mr. Fellows was not likely to help them! He had something he badly wanted to hide, that was certain. *Could* they possibly go hunting in stacks and ricks? The farmers wouldn't be at all pleased.

Fatty told the others about his escapade of the night before. They laughed delightedly.

"Oh, Fatty!" said Bets. "I never knew any one like you in my life. And I never shall. There's just nothing you're scared of doing."

"I was a bit scared of old Goon just now," said Fatty. "Honestly he looked like an angry bull. I don't blame him. I must be pretty annoying to him. I was jolly glad when Buster came flying out!"

"Wuff," said Buster, thumping his tail approvingly.

"Do you think Mr. Goon has got that sack of yours out of the river yet?" said Daisy. "Whatever will he say when he finds it is full of stones and bricks! He doesn't know it was you who dumped it there, does he?"

"No. But he'll guess it was when he finds what's in the sack!" grinned Fatty. "You should have seen me heave it in! Old Goon nearly went in after it."

"Do you think he's gone to look for it now?" asked Bets. "He wouldn't leave it too long, would he? Let's go for a walk down to the river and see if he's anywhere about. We can bike down."

"Yes, do let's," said Daisy. "You've been having all the fun, Fatty – we want some now too. I'd just love to see Mr. Goon digging about with a boat-hook and bringing up a sack full of stones and bricks."

"All right. We might as well," said Fatty, getting up. "Walkie – walk, Buster. Come on!"

They got on their bicycles. Pip and Bets had theirs at Larry's, as they had bicycled there that morning. They free-wheeled down the hill towards the river.

Mr. Goon was not there. Fatty spotted an old

boat-man friend of his, painting a boat outside his shed. He put his bicycle by a tree and hailed him.

"Hallo, Spicer! Getting ready for spring weather? It's been pretty cold lately, hasn't it?"

"Ay, that it has," agreed old Spicer, beaming at the five children. He knew them all. "Why aren't you back at school yet?"

"Term hasn't begun," said Fatty. "Are you letting out any boats yet, Spicer? I suppose we couldn't have one this morning?"

"No. I've only got the one ready that you see down there," said Spicer, nodding his head towards a little, freshly painted boat bobbing by the bank.

"Well why can't we have *her*?" demanded Larry, feeling that he would like a good row more than anything else.

"That bobby rang up and asked me to have one ready for him this morning," said Spicer. "What's his name now – Moon?"

"Goon, you mean," said Fatty. He winked at the others. So Goon *was* going to come and jab about in the river for the sack that Fatty had thrown in. Good!

"Ay, Goon. Wants a boat-hook too," said old Spicer, painting a bright red line with a steady brown hand. "Seems like my boat-hooks are popular this morning. He's the second one wants a boat-hook."

Fatty pricked up his ears. "Who's the other fellow who wants a boat-hook?" he asked, wondering if it was Mr. Fellows. Maybe he wanted to fish out a sack himself!

"I never seen him afore," said Spicer. "Big dark fellow – got a scar down his cheek, and something wrong with one eye. Not a nice piece of work at all, he wasn't. He offered me ten bob for the loan of my longest boat-hook – said he wanted specimens of the weeds growing up and down the river for some botanist fellow."

"I see," said Fatty. The man wasn't Fellows, that was certain. Could he be the would-be burglar, the intruder who had caused Fellows to fly out of his house with a bundle of some kind?

The others were all very interested in this piece of news, too. They nodded to Spicer and walked off till he was out of hearing.

"Queer," said Fatty, in a low voice. "I don't believe that yarn about jabbing for weeds at the bottom of the river. Let's see if we can find the fellow."

"Don't let's go too far away," begged Bets. "I don't want to miss Mr. Goon hunting for your sack, Fatty."

"Well, you four go and watch Mr. Goon when he comes – and I'll saunter up the tow-path as soon as I've asked Spicer where the other fellow went," said Fatty. "Perhaps it would be as well if I wasn't here when Goon finds that sack and opens it – he might throw the stones and the bricks at me!"

He went back to ask Spicer in which direction the man with the boat-hook had gone. "I'm interested in water-weeds myself," said Fatty, quite truthfully. There were very few things that Fatty was *not* interested in!

"He went up yonder," said the old boatman, pointing up the tow-path. "He can't have got very far."

Fatty went up the path, leaving the others sitting on a seat just inside Spicer's shed. From there they could easily see when Mr. Goon came down to the boat. They waited expectantly, hoping for some fun.

Fatty wandered up the tow-path, keeping his eyes open for the man that Spicer had described. He soon saw him, coming back down the path. He had a pail with him, out of which water-weed was hanging. Fatty wondered for a moment if the man really was getting weed for a botanist.

Fatty stopped as the man came up to him. "Got any snails in your weed?" he asked, politely. "I want some for my garden pond."

"Get some yourself then," said the man, in a surly tone. He turned his back on Fatty, and looked down into the water.

"Can I help you?" asked Fatty. "I know a bit about water-weeds."

The man turned round, scowling. "I don't like boys who hang round," he said. "You're not wanted, see? Buzz off!"

Fatty didn't buzz off. He merely sauntered on till he came to a clump of thick bushes. He disappeared round them, forced his way into the centre, and parted a few branches to look through. The bushes were of evergreen box, and Fatty was very well hidden.

He saw the man look back as if to see if Fatty was still anywhere near. But there was no boy to be seen, of course. The man went slowly on his way, looking into the water as he went. He came to a stop at last, and into the water went his boat-hook. He jabbed and poked at something and finally lifted it out. Fatty grinned. An old boot! Well, if he was collecting those, there were plenty in the river!

But the old boot went back with a splash and the man went on again, taking a look round every now and again as if to see if Fatty was still about.

He jabbed again, and brought up something that disgusted him. He threw it back quickly. Another jab and up came a mass of weeds. He put some into his pail.

"That's just for show, Mr. Scarred-Cheek," murmured Fatty, peering through the bush. "In case any one is watching you. Are you thinking that Mr. Fellows has thrown the Treasure, whatever it is, into the river? Or are you just a junk-hunter, wanting to make a few shillings on anything you find? No – I think not. Junk-hunters don't pay ten shillings for the loan of a boat-book!"

The man went slowly on down the tow-path. Fatty grew bored. What were the others doing? Had Mr. Goon arrived yet?

Mr. Goon had! To the delight of the four watching children, and of Buster, who had not been allowed to go with Fatty. Mr. Goon had arrived full speed on his bicycle! He had jammed on his brakes, thrown his bicycle against a tree, and yelled to Spicer.

90

"Got that boat ready? And I want the boat-hook too. I'm pressed for time."

"The boat's ready yonder, and the hook's alongside, sir," shouted back Spicer. Goon grunted and went to the gay little boat. He got in and took the oars. The boat-hook lay beside him. Off he went, and soon began to pant with the effort of his rowing.

"Come on," said Larry, jumping up. "Let's go and watch. I'd better carry Buster though, or he might try and leap into his enemy's boat!"

"Let's not go too near till Mr. Goon gets Fatty's sack of stones and bricks," said Bets. "Let's just saunter up and down, and wait till we see him pull up the sack."

"Right," said Larry. So the four of them, with a struggling Buster in Larry's arms, sauntered up and down in the January sunshine. Mr. Goon soon spotted them and exclaimed angrily under his breath:

"Those kids again! Good thing for that fat boy he's not with them. I don't know what I might do to him with a boat-hook ready to hand!"

He rowed to the jetty. He had decided that it would be much easier to drag up the sack from a boat rather than from the jetty. Mr. Goon feared that he might over-balance if he had to bend down and jab about from the high little jetty!

He stopped rowing when he came to the wooden jetty and drew in his oars. He took up the boat-hook and peered down solemnly into the water. His own red face peered back at him. Mr. Goon looked deeper down and tried to see the bulk of a sack somewhere. But the water was very deep just there and try as he would he could not see the bottom.

He looked up at the jetty. Now where had that old fellow been standing when he dropped the sack into the water. Yes – just about there! Mr. Goon began to prod and jab where he thought the sack might be.

He got hold of nothing but water-weeds. He pulled up hundreds of green, slimy strands and exclaimed in annoyance. Weeds, weeds, weeds – where was that sack? He'd find out what that old man had got in his sack if it took him all morning to do it!

Mr. Goon got very hot jabbing here and there. He suddenly sensed somebody looking at him, and glanced up. He frowned. Those kids! Now they had come to watch him! Like mosquitoes they were, always buzzing round him. Pity he couldn't slap them all away!

Ah! What was this? His boat-hook really had got hold of something this time – something fairly solid too – and fairly heavy. This must be the old man's sack! Mr. Goon puffed and panted, heaved and hauled, trying to get up the sack.

It came up with a rush and Mr. Goon nearly fell overboard. The four watching children gasped, and winked at one another. Mr. Goon had got the sack, hurrah! Now what would happen?

They walked right on the jetty to see. Some way off the man with the boat-hook stood, also watching, his attention suddenly caught by Mr. Goon's antics. A little way behind him stood Fatty, ready to dart into Spicer's shed if Goon's anger was too great!

Mr. Goon was so excited that he didn't even notice all these spectators. He heaved the bundle into the boat. Larry looked at it intently. It didn't look to him like a sack. It looked more like a laundry bag or something like that. Was it Fatty's sack that Goon had got – or was it something else?

Goon looked at the dripping bundle. He saw that it was a bag, not a sack, but he didn't worry about that. He had only seen the bundle on Fatty's back by moonlight. Bag or sack, he was absolutely certain that this was what the old man had thrown into the river last night!

He undid the string that tied the neck. He opened it wide. He put in his hand, wondered what he was going to find – the result of several burglaries he had no doubt!

Ah, a big stone. That would be to weight it down – and another stone – and another. Goon fished them out rapidly and tossed them into the water. Splash!

The watching children now felt sure that this was

Fatty's sack – look at all the stones! But now Goon was rummaging deep in the bundle. His face took on a puzzled look. He couldn't feel anything except soft, dripping clothes – or what felt like clothes.

He drew one out. He shook it – and amazement spread over his face. It was a small red coat! He put it into the bottom of the boat and delved into the bundle again.

A pair of blue trousers – long ones, but far too small for a normal boy! Goon began to snort. He pulled out various things one by one – a red belt – a blue tie – a blue cap with a red button on top – a pair of socks – and, finally, a pair of small red shoes with laces.

Goon couldn't make them out. Why should an old man in the night carry these things about in a sack? It didn't make sense. Why had the old fellow been so determined that he, Goon, shouldn't see into the sack, or take it?

Goon looked at the array of small garments, and his face grew purple once more. That boy! That toad of a boy! *He* must have been the old man! He had spoofed Goon with a sack of dolls' clothes! Yes, that's what they were, dolls' clothes! That girl, Daisy, must have been in the trick too – she must have lent them to him – stuffed them into the sack ready to trick Goon into thinking the old man had stolen something, and to make Goon follow him!

"Gah," said Goon, in angry disgust. "Didn't he run like a hare when he'd dumped these into the water? I thought that was queer at the time. That boy was the fellow who talked to the watchmen, and he was the old man too. He's too bad to be true, that fat boy. I'll not keep my hands off him this time – I'll get him, and I'll stuff these things down his horrible neck, so I will. If I lose me job I'll do it!"

Goon shoved the things back into the bag again. He was boiling with rage, and his hands shook. He'd report that Toad to the Chief. He'd make the Chief do something about him. He'd go round and complain to Mr. and Mrs. Trotteville. The things he'd tell them about that fat boy of theirs!"

He took up the oars and rowed away from the jetty, muttering to himself. The four children, seeing him look so fierce, decided to go back and warn Fatty. They set off on the towing-path at top speed.

They came up to Fatty, who was grinning. He had been too far away to see what had been taken out of the bundle. All he had seen were the three stones being tossed into the water. He had thought, of course, that they were some of the stones he had put into his own sack.

"Fatty! Goon's got some other sack, not yours!" said Daisy, in an urgent voice. "It was full of clothes – dolls' clothes, they looked like. I'm sure he thinks you put them there to spoof him. You'd better go quick before he comes! He's SIMPLY FURIOUS!"

A Wonderful Scrimmage – and a Discovery

Fatty listened. He was suddenly very interested. *Clothes!* That was a funny thing for any one to dump into the river in a sack. Goon had got the wrong sack – he would, of course.

"I'll pop into old Spicer's shed, I think," said Fatty. "I'd like to see what Goon does when he lands. He won't spot me in the shed."

He disappeared into the big, dark shed and sat down on an upturned boat. The four children turned to watch Goon rowing nearer and nearer. The scarred-faced man also watched, looking very interested in the rowing policeman. He had given back his boat-hook and now had only his pail of water-weed.

Goon, still purple in the face, drew in to the bank. He threw the mooring-rope over a post and clambered out, the boat rocking dangerously under his weight. He picked up the bag into which he had stuffed the wet clothes.

He looked at the four children nearby, scowling.

"Where's that fat friend of yours? I want him. I've got a few things to say to him!"

"What fat friend?" asked Larry innocently. Goon's scowl became even more ferocious.

"You know who I mean – that Toad of a boy!" spluttered the angry policeman.

The old boatman heard him. He was still painting his boat, and looked amused at Mr. Goon.

"He's in there," he said, pointing to the shed. "What you going to do to him, Mr. Goon?"

"In there?" said Mr. Goon, delighted. Aha! Now he'd show that boy something!

He strode into the dark shed, determined to do or die this time. He'd stuff these things down that fat boy's neck till he yelled. He'd smother him with them! That would teach him to play tricks on him again!

Fatty was taken by surprise when Goon walked in. Larry shouted a warning just too late. Goon was on Fatty before he knew it.

And then Mr. Goon had the time of his life! He caught hold of the seated Fatty, held him in an iron grip, and began to stuff the wet, dripping garments down his neck, wrenching open his collar, tearing his shirt, but not caring in the least.

Fatty could do nothing. He was half choked, to begin with, by having things forced down the front of his neck, and Mr. Goon was extremely solid and strong. He struggled and heaved, and finally fell off the boat he was sitting on, landing on the earth-floor of the shed. Mr. Goon fell on top of him.

All the breath was squeezed out of poor Fatty. He could hardly even gasp with the policeman's enormous form on top of him. And still Goon went on relentlessly pushing everything down Fatty's neck! Trousers, coat, socks, cap, shoes, one by one down they went. Goon was absolutely determined to punish Fatty this time!

Larry ran at Goon and so did Pip. They tried to pull the furious policeman away, and Daisy and Bets rained blows on his back which he hardly felt. Old Spicer heard

Mr. Goon held Fatty in an iron grip

the noise and came in, astonished. He stopped, gaping, when he saw the scrimmage.

The man with the water-weed came too. He watched with great interest, very great interest indeed.

At last everything was down poor Fatty's neck. He felt wet and uncomfortable, breathless and bruised. Mr. Goon stood up, panting, feeling uncommonly satisfied with himself.

"You got what's been coming to you for a very long time," he panted. "Now just you stop poking your nose into things, Mister Nosey-Parker! Stuffing that sack with rubbishy dolls' clothes, and stuffing me up too, making me think you were a bad old man with stolen goods. Ho! Now *you've* been stuffed up good and proper!"

"Mr. Goon!" said old Spicer in a shocked voice. "You're a policeman! You can't do things like this – to a boy too!"

Gah!" said Mr. Goon, rudely. "You go and boil your head, Spicer. That boy won't complain of what I've done, I know that! And for why – because he's been plaguing me night and day, and interfering with the Law. If he complains of me, I'll complain of him – but he won't! He's got a guilty conscience, he has, He's a Bad Lot, and one of these days he'll come to No Good."

"Mr. Goon," said Fatty, sitting up and trying to look as dignified as he could, with dripping garments down his neck and hanging out of his collar. "Mr. Goon. I give you my word of honour I didn't spoof you with these things. I've never seen them before in my life. You owe me an apology."

"I owe you a lot of things," said Mr. Goon, "yes, a whole lot. But not an apology. You put those things into that sack to spoof me, made me waste half a morning for nothing, and you got what you deserved – you got them in the neck! And what's more you can keep them! Or give them back to that girl to dress up her dolls!"

And, with a perfectly marvellous snort, Mr. Goon marched out of the shed. He bumped into the man with the water-weed.

"Excuse me," began the man, "I'd just like to know where . . ."

Mr. Goon snorted at him rudely and walked past, shoving him out of the way. He was feeling fine. Oh, Mr. Goon was on top of the world at that moment. He could have put the Chief Inspector in his place, too, with a few well-chosen words – if only he had been there. But he wasn't – which was perhaps just as well for the triumphant Goon.

"Oh, Fatty, Fatty, are you hurt?" said Bets, in tears. She was very scared. "Oh, Fatty, are you all right?" She began to sob.

"I'm fine, Bets," Fatty assured her, getting up and feeling himself all over. "I just feel like a rubber ball with a few dents in me. My word, Goon's a weight. Don't cry, Bets, please don't. It was a wonderful fight."

"It wasn't, it wasn't," sobbed Bets. "I hated it. I hate Mr. Goon. I shall tell the Chief Inspector."

"No. Goon only got back at me for all the maddening things I've done to him," said Fatty, relieved to find that he had no bones broken. "He'll feel better now. You were wonderful to come to my rescue, Bets. Now please don't cry any more. That upsets me much more than Goon's attack!" He put his arm round Bets.

"Cry-baby," interposed Pip, in his nice, brotherly way. "Shut up, Bets. Don't make a fool of yourself."

"Let her alone, Pip," said Fatty. "She's really scared – and I don't wonder. Goon looked a pretty nasty bit of work when he flung himself at me. But what a peculiar thing to do – to stuff these things down my neck! Ugh! They're frightfully wet and smelly."

"Let's get back home and fish them out," said Larry, seeing two or three interested children coming up on their way home from morning school. "Come on, Fatty. We'll get our bikes."

Spicer grinned good-bye and patted the red-eyed Bets as she passed. The water-weed man stood silently watching. The school children nudged one another and grinned. Fatty really looked very peculiar just then.

They got on their bicycles. Fatty had recovered now.

He felt a new respect for Goon. Fancy him thinking of such a thing – and doing it too! Fatty shivered as he felt some cold, wet drops running down his chest.

They rode to Fatty's house and went to his shed. They locked the door. Fatty looked round. "I say – where's old Buster? He never came to my rescue!"

"He went off with old Spicer's terrier," said Larry, suddenly remembering. "Spicer said his dog would show Buster how to catch rabbits in the fields behind the boat-house, and off they went. I never thought another thing about him! Things got so exciting that I forgot about old Buster."

"Well, I do think he might have come to my help," said Fatty, half-vexed. "He'd have enjoyed it too – free bites at any portion of Mr. Goon that he fancied!"

"He'll come home when he's found out that, as usual, rabbits aren't really catchable," said Daisy. "Oh, Fatty, you *are* wet. You'd better strip off your coat and shirt and vest and put on dry ones."

"Larry, you go indoors and get me some," said Fatty. "Mother's out, so she won't want to know what you're doing, carrying my underwear about!"

Larry disappeared. Fatty took off his coat, pulled off his shirt, and stripped off his vest. It was then easy to get rid of the damp, smelly things that Goon had put down his neck. Fatty looked at them in distaste.

"Nasty wet things! Who could have been such an idiot as to dump dolls' clothes into a sack, weight them with stones, and sink them in the river. It doesn't make sense."

"I'll take them to the dustbin," said Daisy, gathering them up. "That's the best place for them."

She lumped them together, trousers, coat, tie shoes, socks, belt, shirt, everything – and went out to the dustbin. They heard her put on the lid and then back she came again.

Larry came in too with some clean, dry clothes. Fatty was about to put them on when he wriggled.

"I've still got something down me somewhere," he said. "I can feel a nasty, cold, wet patch on my tummy.

99

Perhaps it's a wet sock. Wait a minute – I really must get it."

He wriggled his hand down and caught hold of something. "Got it," he said. "I thought I felt one last thing. It's a red sock."

He flung it down on the floor of the shed and then began to dress himself rapidly in dry clothes. Bets bent down to pick up the little red woollen thing. It was limp and shapeless.

"It's not a sock," she said. "It's a glove – a little red glove."

Fatty swung his head round quickly and incredulously. Bets had got the little glove and was pulling the fingers straight. Fatty snatched it from her.

"A little red glove. *Another* one!" he said, jubilantly. "The pair to the one I've got in my pocket! Where is it? Look! Exactly the same!"

He pulled the first little red glove out of his trousers pocket, and put it beside the one that Mr. Goon had stuffed down his back. They were an exact match!

Every one stared at the two gloves. How very, very extraordinary!

"But – what does it mean?" asked Daisy, at last. "You found that first glove in Mr. Fellows' house."

"And Goon stuffed the second one down my neck! He's given us the biggest clue yet!" said Fatty. "Oh, dear, dear old Goon – you've nearly solved the mystery for us by stuffing things down my neck!"

That Night

There was a silence after this rather peculiar statement. Nobody could quite follow it. What did Fatty mean?

"Don't stand round me looking daft like that!" said Fatty. "Don't you *see* what this means? It means that the bag of clothes that Goon hooked up is the bundle that Mr. Fellows rushed off with and threw into the river

– to hide! The bundle that the other fellow was after, for some reason or other!"

"But how do you know?" asked Daisy.

"Well, because I picked up one of the red gloves in a corner of the landing in Fellows' house!" said Fatty, impatiently. "He must have pushed everything quickly into a bag to rush off to hide it somewhere – but one of the little gloves dropped out!"

"Oh – I *see*," said Larry. "Yes – your red glove does prove that this bundle was the one that Fellows rushed off with in such a hurry. But, Fatty – why are these dolls' clothes so important?"

"We'll get them and see," said Fatty. "Daisy, go and haul them out of the dustbin again. We'll go through them carefully. There must be *some*thing to tell us why they are apparently of such importance."

Daisy and Larry went off to get them – but just as they were going back to the shed with them, they heard the voice of Mrs. Trotteville's cook.

"You children! Do you know it's nearly half-past one! Your mother's been telephoning here for you, Miss Daisy, and so has Mrs. Hilton for Master Pip! And Master Frederick's lunch has been waiting for him for a long time."

"Oh, blow, blow, blow!" groaned Larry. "Just when we were going to do something REALLY exciting!" He hurried to the shed and told the others.

Fatty looked longingly at the bundle of wet clothes. "Well – we must wait till this afternoon. Anyway the clothes will be drier by then. I'll take them up to my room and dry them by the electric fire."

"Promise you won't examine them till we come back?" said Bets urgently.

"I promise," said Fatty. "Go on, now, all of you – and I hope you don't get into a row."

They all left at top speed, fearing that they certainly *would* get into a row.

They did. Two really angry mothers met them at their doors. "A quarter to two! What *are* you thinking of?"

The dreadful result was that not one of the four was

allowed to go down to Fatty's that afternoon, nor even to leave the house! Larry and Daisy sat disconsolately in their playroom and Pip and Bets sat in theirs. Fatty waited till three o'clock and then telephoned. He wasn't even allowed to *speak* to the others.

Larry's mother was cross. "You should really not keep Larry and Daisy so late," she said. Fatty apologized humbly and gloomily.

Mrs. Hilton said a good deal more. Fatty felt even humbler when she had finished. He could hear Bets' voice calling to her mother at the end.

"Mother! MOTHER! Ask Fatty if Buster is back, please, please ask him."

Mrs. Hilton asked him. "Yes – tell Bets he arrived an hour ago, covered in sand and awfully hungry," said Fatty. "I shan't let him go off with old Spicer's dog again."

He heard Mrs. Hilton's receiver click down. He turned and glared at Buster who was sitting nearby. looking very guilty.

"To think you deserted me when Goon attacked me!" said Fatty. "Shameful dog! To go rabbiting when your master is in danger! Brrrrrrrr!"

Fatty went up to his room and looked longingly at all the things he had put in front of the fire. They were perfectly dry now. How he longed to examine them! But no, he had promised, and it simply didn't occur to Fatty to break such a promise. He bundled all the clothes into a drawer.

The rest of the day was extremely dull. The Mystery was at a standstill till the others could come and look at the curious clothes. Buster was still feeling guilty and was not at all lively. It began to pour with rain. And now Fatty's bruises were beginning to come up nicely. He examined them carefully.

"A good little lot," he said to himself. "But not so big as Goon would like to see."

The other Find-Outers were not allowed out at all that day. They sat and moped and sulked. How maddening to be kept in just when they really had got somewhere! Bets and Pip talked about the dolls' clothes.

"Funny that they should be important enough for some one to break into Mr. Fellows' house and turn the place upside down for them," said Pip.

"I bet Mr. Fellows will be going out with a boat-hook too, to try and get them back," said Bets.

"Queer that those dolls' clothes should be for a boy not for a girl," said Daisy to Larry.

"How mad Goon would be to know that he had made a present of such an enormous clue to Fatty," said Larry. "I guess nobody has ever had a clue stuffed down their neck before. Just like Goon!"

They all went to bed early. Both Larry's mother and Pip's were still annoyed, and only Fatty's mother was good-tempered that day – but that was because she had been out to lunch, and hadn't been kept waiting like the others!

She was very surprised at Fatty's bruises. One came out on his right cheek, another on his chin and one on his left hand. There were others she couldn't see, of course.

"How in the world did you get all those bruises?" she asked Fatty.

"Oh – just rolling about," said Fatty, airily, and changed the subject quickly. He went to bed early and read, with Buster under the eiderdown beside him. A very contrite and humble Buster, who was now quite forgiven.

Fatty was tired. "More 'aftermath'," he supposed. He switched off his light early and fell into a sound sleep. His parents were up in town that evening, having driven up to a theatre and a dance afterwards. They would not be back until about one o'clock in the morning, perhaps later.

At half-past ten the whole house was in darkness except for a small light on in the hall. The two maids were in bed and asleep. Buster slept soundly too. So did Fatty.

He was suddenly awakened by Buster barking loudly.

WUFF, WUFF, WUFF! He sat up with a jerk and turned on the light. A quarter to one.

"Shut up, Buster. It's only Mother and Dad you can hear!" said Fatty, sleepily. "Do shut up. Surely you know the sound of their car by now!"

But Buster wouldn't stop. He leapt from the bed to the floor and barked frantically. Fatty threw a book at him.

"Shut up, I tell you! It's only Mother coming home. You know she and Dad are out. Come here, Buster."

Buster took not the slightest notice. Fatty thought there really might be something the matter. He jumped out of bed, pulled on his dressing-gown and opened the door. A frightened voice called to him.

"Master Frederick? Is that you? Why is Buster barking? Is there some one in the house?"

"I expect it's just my parents coming back," said Fatty. "You go to bed again. Buster's gone downstairs at top speed, so you may be sure if there's any one down there he'll be after them!"

Buster was still barking frantically somewhere downstairs. Fatty decided to explore. He was about to go downstairs when he caught sight of his mother's bedroom. The door was open and the landing light streamed into it. It was in utter confusion!

"Gosh!" said Fatty, switching on the light. "Look at that. Burglars! While we were all asleep!"

He looked in his father's dressing-room and into the guest-room. Both had had their drawers and cupboards rifled and turned out. Fatty ran downstairs. Buster was standing by an open window in the sitting-room, barking madly.

"It's no good barking *now*, Buster," said Fatty, glancing round the sitting-room, which was in as much muddle and confusion as the other rooms. "The thief is gone – he must have been about to come into my room when you heard him and awoke. He's gone out of the same window he came in by. I wonder what he's taken. Not Mother's jewellery, I hope."

There came the sound of a car up the drive. It was

his parents returning home. Fatty heaved a sigh of relief. Now they could take matters in hand.

Mr. and Mrs. Trotteville were horrified when they came indoors and saw all the confusion in so many rooms. Mrs. Trotteville rapidly looked through her jewellery, fur coats, and silver. They were all intact.

"It's queer," she said, after about twenty minutes' search. "I can't see that *any*thing has been taken. Even this pearl necklace I left on my dressing-table hasn't been taken. What did the thief come for?"

Fatty suddenly knew! The intruder must have been the same one who had searched Mr. Fellows' house. And he had been looking for the same thing – the dolls' clothes! But why – why – why?

Fatty raced up to his room to see if they were still safe. Yes – they were there in the drawer into which he had thrown them. What a blessing he hadn't left them down in the kitchen to dry, as he had first thought of doing. He had only taken them up to his room so that awkward questions would not be asked by any one who saw such strange things drying on the kitchen airer!

But how did the burglar know that the clothes were now in Fatty's house? Fatty soon thought that one out. The man with the water-weed! He had been looking on while Mr. Goon had stuffed the wet clothes down Fatty's neck. *He* had been looking for them that morning too – but it was Goon who had found them – and thrown them away on Fatty!

How wild the water-weed man must have been when he saw something he badly wanted being stuffed down a boy's neck! He must have asked old Spicer who Fatty was and where he lived – and then he had come to try and get the clothes back that night.

Fatty looked at the clothes in the drawer. "There's something extraordinarily valuable about you," he said solemnly. "Maybe we'll find out tomorrow."

He heard his mother talking to his father. "Are you going to phone for the police?"

"No, I'm not," said his father's voice. "I don't want that flat-footed policeman stamping all over my house late at night! There's nothing gone, as far as I can see. We'll let Mr. Goon sleep in peace!"

"Thank goodness," said Fatty, sliding into bed. "I just don't feel like seeing Goon again tonight."

Examining the Clothes

To Fatty's relief his father decided next day not to inform Mr. Goon of the attempted robbery at all. Mr. Trotteville had no great opinion of Mr. Goon, and was not disposed to waste a morning with him.

"He'd ask asinine questions, and waste everybody's time," said Mr. Trotteville. "Just have new fastenings put on all the windows, my dear, and another bolt on the front and back door. And perhaps Buster had better sleep downstairs."

Buster had other views, however. He had heard suggestions like this before, but however firmly he was put into a basket in the hall and told to be on guard, he was invariably to be found lying on Fatty's bed in the morning. As Mr. Trotteville said, it was most extraordinary the way that Buster could find his way through a closed bedroom door!

Fatty telephoned the others. "Come on down as soon as you can," he said. "I've news. We've had robbers in the night. No – nothing taken, as far as I can see. Old Buster drove them off. Buck up and come down."

They met down in the shed at the bottom of Fatty's garden. Fatty kept a good lookout for the water-weed man, as he called him, when he took the clothes down to the shed. He wouldn't have been surprised to have him pounce on him from behind a tree! However, Buster trotted happily in front, and nothing untoward happened at all. Fatty was safely ensconced in the shed when the others came tapping at the door.

He shut the door and locked it. He pulled the curtains over the windows, and lighted the little oil-lamp so that they were not in complete darkness.

"Why all the mystery?" asked Daisy, surprised. "Going to do conjuring tricks, or something?"

"No. But that water-weed man is somewhere around, I bet," said Fatty. "And I don't want him peeping in at the window while we're examining those clothes. He's dead keen on getting them. He's made two break-ins already in different houses to get them. I don't want to have to give them up at the point of a pistol."

"Gracious, Fatty!" said Bets, in alarm.

"It's all right, Bets," said Fatty. "Now, before we start – any one want to see my bruises? I've got some beauties."

Every one wanted to see them, and they certainly were magnificent. Fatty always bruised very well, and was very ready to exhibit his best ones.

"And now for the clothes," said Fatty, taking them out of the box he had put them in. "Use your eyes well – there's obviously Something we mustn't miss! Now – the trousers first!"

He shook out the blue trousers. They were long ones, with little buttons at the top. "No pockets," said Fatty. "Don't dolls' clothes ever have pockets, Bets?"

"Oh yes, sometimes," said Bets. "Aren't they dear little trousers – a boy doll would look nice in those. Let me have them, Fatty."

Bets took them. She turned them inside out. There was nothing that would tell them anything – they were just trousers with buttons. Bets passed them round to the others, and then Fatty put them down.

"Red belt for the trousers," he said, and passed it round. "Quite ordinary. A little brass buckle, a bit rusty – due to the river water, I suppose."

It was duly examined. Then came the socks. Those were turned inside out too. Bets hunted for any name marked on them, but there wasn't one.

"Dolls never have their names marked on their clothes, silly," said Pip, when Bets remarked why she was looking so carefully.

"Mine do," said Bets. "I borrowed Mother's marking tape and ink, and I've marked all my biggest doll's clothes with her name – Pamela Mary. Anyway, you needn't laugh at me! Who painted names on the front of his engines? The Flying Scotsman! The Night Flyer. The . . ."

"That's enough from you, young Bets," said her brother. "Pass the shoes, Fatty. Gosh, aren't they small!"

"Well, they're small for a child, but big for a doll," said Fatty. "Very nice shoes, though – strong and well made – not like the usual doll's shoes. These have real laces in too."

"I suppose these clothes *couldn't* belong to some child – some little dwarf child, say?" said Larry.

"Well – I suppose they might," said Fatty. "But for the life of me I can't see why they're so important, whether they belong to a doll or a child! Not worth breaking into two houses for, anyway!"

Bets undid the laces and did them up again. They really were nice little shoes! She showed one to Buster. He sniffed at it.

"Buster – who does it belong to?" said Bets. "Go on, tell us! Surely you can tell by the smell! Whose smell is it?"

"Wuff!" said Buster, and pawed at the shoe. Bets dodged it away, and Buster sprang at it. He got it in his mouth and ran off with it triumphantly. He stuffed it into a corner and sat down on it, as if to say, "It's mine now."

"Bring it here, Buster," said Bets. "It's ours!" Buster took it into his mouth and ran round the shed to hide it somewhere. He was in a silly mood that morning and had already run off with Daisy's handkerchief and Fatty's pencil.

"Don't take any notice of him," said Fatty. "He's got one of his show-off fits on. Probably feels very grand because he scared off a burglar last night. All right, Buster, be an idiot if you want to. Look – here's the coat, complete with buttons and collar!"

That was examined too. Fatty ran his hands down

the lining. Could there be anything hidden there that might be of value. No – he could feel nothing.

Every one examined it solemnly. It was a well made little coat, of good material, strong and very little worn.

"The longer we look at these things the more puzzled I feel," said Fatty. "Who wore them – and why should they have been stolen. At least, I suppose they *were* stolen. . . ."

"By Mr. Fellows, do you mean?" asked Larry. "But how do we know he stole them?"

"Well, why should he have them and hide them as he did?" said Fatty. "What beats me is why they are apparently of such importance. Here's the tie, look – and the cap. Nice cap. Very nice indeed. Quite a cheeky cap, in fact!"

He set it on his large head at a comical angle. Bets laughed. "You look frightful, Fatty. Take it off."

"Even battier than usual," said Pip, and got a punch from Fatty. Buster, always ready for a battle, flung himself on the two boys, barking. Fatty sat up and pushed him away.

"Where's that shoe?" he said, severely. "You bring it back here, and we'll admit you into the family circle again. And what have you done with my pencil? If you've chewed the end off, you can count it as your dinner, because you won't get any more!"

Buster retired to his corner, his tongue hanging out. Bets thought he looked sweet. She liked him when he was "showing-off!"

"Is that all the clothes?" asked Daisy, examining the cap carefully, when Fatty handed it round. "I simply can't see anything out of the ordinary about these things at all – except that they're better made and stronger than ordinary dolls' clothes. I can't think why they are important."

"Neither can I. But they must be," said Fatty. He gazed at the pile of clothes rather gloomily. "I wouldn't a bit mind Goon having stuffed them down my neck if only they'd prove to be really worth while – help us with this rather peculiar mystery. Though I'm beginning to think we may be making a mountain out of a molehill, and that it's not a mystery at all."

"Well, we've only got two or three days more to solve it," said Bets. "I don't think I could *bear* to go back to school without knowing the solution of this queer little mystery. Do you suppose we ought to take these dolls' clothes back to Mr. Fellows?"

"Well, yes – I suppose we ought," said Fatty. "I actually hadn't thought of that. We could ask him what *his* explanation is – we might find out something after all! We'll take them this afternoon. He'll be astonished to see them, I bet! He probably thinks they're still safe in the river!"

"I do WISH we'd managed to find some clue hidden in the clothes," said Bets. "I'm sure there must be. Let me go through them just once more, Fatty, before you put them away."

"You think you might discover something that all five of us couldn't see?" said Pip, scornfully. "What a hope!"

"It's always a good thing to have another check on anything if you feel you must," said Fatty, handing the bundle of clothes to Bets. "They're all there, Bets – except the shoe that Buster took. Hey, Buster, bring back the shoe, old fellow."

But before Buster could do as he was told, Bets gave a loud exclamation that made every one jump. She was examining the little red coat, and she looked up, her eyes shining.

"Look – we missed this – a little white handkerchief embroidered with daisies – and it's got a name embroidered on it too – very small!"

"Where was it?" asked Fatty, almost snatching the tiny hanky.

"There's a very small pocket here inside the coat-cuff," said Bets, showing the others. "So well hidden that none of us saw it. Fatty, what's the name on the hanky?"

Fatty spread out the tiny hanky so that all the Find-Outers could see the little daisies on it and the name that was embroidered all round them, making a circle of the letters.

Fatty spelt it out. "E-U-R-Y-C-L-E-S. Eurycles! What a name."

"Never heard it in my life," said Larry. "It's Greek, isn't it?"

"Yes. Greek," said Fatty. "Wait – wait – I've heard it before. Who was Eurycles? I'm remembering – yes. I'm remembering. EURYCLES! Of course – I remember now. What a clue!"

Mr. Eurycles – and a talk with Goon

The others stared at Fatty in excitement. What was the clue? Who was Eurycles the Greek? And why did it matter who he was?

"Listen," said Fatty. "Eurycles was a Greek who lived ages ago – but he happened to be a very well-known Greek, because he had a peculiar gift – he was a ventriloquist! He was such a jolly good one that he's never been forgotten, and he had dozens of pupils."

"I thought ventriloquists were all modern," said Daisy, in astonishment. "I mean – I thought it was something that people had thought of in the last century, say."

"Good gracious no – it's a very old art," said Fatty. "It was well known in Greece – and all kinds of nations have practised it – the Zulus, for instance – and the Eskimos. And Eurycles the Greek was a very fine ventriloquist. I read about him when I was teaching myself to ventriloquise and to throw my voice to a distance."

"Yes – but why should this doll's hanky have an old Greek ventriloquist's name on it?" said Daisy. "And why is it important?" I simply don't understand, Fatty. Do explain."

"Now listen," said Fatty, thrilled. "When hankies are embroidered with somebody's name, that name usually belongs to the owner of the hanky, doesn't it? Right,

111

either the one who owned that hanky and wore these clothes was called Eurycles – or his *master* was. Mr. Eurycles – what could he be but a ventriloquist, and what could these clothes belong to but his talking doll!"

The others followed this with interest, and at the end Pip exclaimed:

"Of course, of course, of course – why didn't we think of it! The clothes were worn by a big doll belonging to a ventriloquist – that's why they are a bit smaller than a child's and rather big for an ordinary doll, and that's why they are very well made."

"Yes. And I bet he is owned by some one whose stage name is Mr. Eurycles, after the old Greek ventriloquist," said Fatty, jubilantly. "I see daylight at last!"

"Well, it's more than I do," said Larry. "What kind of daylight can you see? It's true that we think we know who the clothes are worn by, and probably the name of the man who owns the doll who wears the clothes . . ."

"That lived in the house that Jack built!" said Daisy, with a giggle.

"Well," said Fatty. "We've only got to find Mr. Eurycles and ask him why the clothes are so important – why they were in Mr. Fellows' custody, why they were important enough for some one to try and steal them twice, and why Mr. Fellows fled out in the night to dump them in the river? Once Mr. Eurycles tells us that, the mystery is solved!"

"But how do we find Mr. Eurycles?" said Pip, after a pause. "It might take ages. And we're going back to school so soon."

There was a silence, which deepened into gloom. Only Fatty remained confident.

"I'll telephone the place that sells things for conjurers and ventriloquists," he said. "They'll soon tell me if there's a Mr. Eurycles."

"Or Mr. Fellows might tell us," said Daisy, suddenly.

"Yes. He might," said Fatty. "And he might not. If he's stolen the clothes himself from Mr. Eurycles, he won't want to say very much. I'll tell you what we'll do – we'll take the clothes to him this afternoon and see his face when we show them to him – and we'll fire a few questions at him before he's got time to recover from his surprise."

"Right," said Larry. "Well, let's put them away till we're ready to take them. I'm sure I heard your mother in the garden just now, Fatty, and she might want to know why we're all playing with dolls' clothes if she walks into the shed!"

The clothes were bundled anyhow into a box. Fatty shut down the lid.

"There's the hanky, look," said Bets, holding it out to him. "It's such a dear little hanky. I suppose I couldn't keep it in my pocket till we take the clothes to Mr. Fellows, Fatty? I won't blow my nose on it."

"Yes. You keep it," said Fatty. "And congratulations on finding the one thing that led us to the right solution! We're well on the way to solving the whole thing now! Jolly good, Bets!"

Bets blushed, and put the little hanky into her pocket. It *was* a bit of luck finding that tiny pocket in the sleeve of the little red coat!

"I vote we go and have some hot chocolate again at the dairy," said Fatty. "And some macaroons if they've made any fresh ones. I feel just like three or four macaroons."

"Yes – all gooey and crunchy," said Pip. "I suddenly feel like a macaroon too. Come on. You do have some bright ideas, Fatty."

They went out of the shed with Buster delightedly prancing round their ankles. Fatty locked the door, and they all went up the path to the garden gate.

They bicycled to the dairy with Buster running beside them. Fatty thought it would be good for him to have a quick run. "Take off some of his fat," he said. "A fat Scottie is an offence to the eye. Do you hear that, Buster?"

"Wuff, wuff," panted Buster. Bets giggled.

"He says that a fat master is also an offence to the eye!" she said. Fatty stared at her in amazement.

"Bets! You've got very bright – and very cheeky all of a sudden!"

"I know. It just popped into my head," said Bets, with another giggle. "Sorry, Fatty. Look out, you nearly wobbled over Buster."

"There's Goon," said Larry suddenly. "Look – coming round the corner on his bike. Let's hope he doesn't hang around us."

"He's probably hoping we shan't hang round *him*," said Fatty, getting off his bicycle and putting it outside the dairy window. "Come on in. I smell fresh macaroons!"

They all trooped in. The little shop-woman beamed at them. They were very good customers indeed! Children always were. They ate twice as much as any grown-up who came into her shop!

"Hot chocolate for every one, please – and macaroons," said Fatty, sitting down at a table.

"Five macaroons?" asked the shop-woman, with a twinkle.

"Gosh, no – ten, to start with, just so we won't look too greedy," said Fatty, with a grin.

"They're new made," said the little woman, warningly. "Don't you eat too many."

"Are you trying to put us off your magnificent macaroons?" said Fatty. "What a hope! Ten, please – just to start with."

Mr. Goon came in. He was looking worried. "You all right?" he said to Fatty, in an off-hand voice. Fatty stared at him, amazed.

"Why this sudden concern for my health, Mr. Goon?" he said. "Why shouldn't I be all right? Are *you* in good health? Let me see your tongue. Say ninety-nine – or one hundred and sixty-two and a half, if you like."

"Perhaps he's feeling sorry he behaved so badly yesterday," said Bets, unexpectedly, giving Mr. Goon a really fierce glare. "Stuffing things down people's necks. Giving them enormous bruises."

"Shut up, young Bets," said Fatty. "It was a good scrum while it lasted." He looked at Mr. Goon, puzzled.

114

It wasn't like the bad-tempered policeman to feel concerned about anything he had done to Fatty. There was something behind this. Fatty wondered what it was.

The hot chocolate and macaroons arrived. Fatty threw another glance at Mr. Goon. He was standing looking round the dairy, as if he had something to say and didn't know how to begin. What *could* have happened?

"Hot cocoa, sir – and a bun or macaroon?" said the little shop-woman. "Just new made."

"No, thanks – er – well, yes, I think I will," said Goon, changing his mind suddenly. He sat down at the table next to the children's. He really did look worried.

He made the five children feel so uncomfortable that they fell silent. Buster was tied to the leg of the table, but even he didn't seem inclined to bait Mr. Goon that morning.

Mr. Goon suddenly cleared his throat with an enormous noise. "Now he's going to talk!" whispered Pip.

"Er – you heard from Chief Inspector Jenks lately?" blurted out Goon, suddenly.

"Not a word," said Fatty promptly. Goon at once looked vastly relieved. He edged his chair a little nearer to the children's table.

"See here," he said to Fatty, "I want to talk with you. Friendly-like."

"You mean you won't fling yourself at me and stuff things down my neck and squash me as if you were a garden-roller?" said Fatty, attacking a macaroon. "In a word – friendly-like."

"It's like this," said Goon, with his mouth full. "You see – well – it's like this, Master Frederick. Er, well . . ."

"Get on, Mr. Goon, and say what you want to say," said Fatty, beginning to be impatient. "Good gracious – you sound as if you can't say Gah to a Goose this morning."

Bets gave a sudden giggle. Gah to a Goose. That was just like Fatty.

Goon made a great effort and came to the point. "It's like this," he said. "You remember that time we were in

Goon edged his chair nearer to the children's table

Mr. Fellows' house together – the time you *said* you were looking for the kitten?"

"Yes," said Fatty.

"Well, do you remember hearing a dog growl and a pig grunt, and a man groaning?" said Mr. Goon, earnestly.

"The one who longed for his Auntie?" said Fatty. "I've often wondered if she ever went to comfort him. Yes, I remember. Why? What about it?"

"Well, I made out a report for the Chief Inspector, see?" said Goon. "Put it all in, pig and all. And the man who said he never did it and kept on about his Auntie."

"Yes. Do get to the point," said Fatty. "I can hardly wait!"

"I sent in the report," said Goon, miserably. "And the Chief don't believe a word of it. Not one word! He wasn't half snorty about it over the phone this morning. So I told him you were there too, Master Frederick, and heard the whole lot. I said you were a proper witness of all the facts, though I hadn't said so in the report."

"I see," said Fatty, at once understanding not only Goon's gloom but also his sudden anxiety to be on good terms with him! "You want me to back you up, I suppose?"

"Yes. You see, you did hear all those noises too, didn't you?" said Goon anxiously.

"I bet you exaggerated everything in your report," said Fatty. "I'll back you up in any facts, but not in any exaggerations, Goon. That's flat."

Goon drummed his fat fingers on the table top. "I may have let meself go a bit," he admitted. "I don't rightly remember. But the thing is – you were with me, Master Frederick, and you did hear things, didn't you?"

"All right, Goon. But I don't see why you had to go and write a fairy tale about the silly happenings in Mr. Fellows' house," said Fatty, crossly. He was beginning to feel distinctly uncomfortable himself. Suppose the Inspector demanded full explanations? Fatty would feel extremely small. He could only hope that nothing more would come of this.

"Thanks, Master Frederick," said Goon, breathing more easily. "We've had our scraps, like, and called each other bad names – but I knew I could depend on you to back up the truth. Thanks."

He paid his bill and got up to go. A voice came weakly from the corner of the dairy. "I never did it, I never, I never! I never did it, I . . ."

But Goon was gone – gone like a hare before the hounds. With one horrified glance at the corner he tore out of the shop. Was he being haunted? That voice, that awful voice!

A Dreadful Shock

There was a startled silence. The Voice had come so suddenly, and sounded so pathetic! Then Pip gave Fatty a vigorous punch.

"Gosh, you startled me! You might warn us when you're going to do that, Mr. Eurycles!"

"I swallowed half my macaroon," complained Larry. "You made me jump so."

"Oh, Fatty – how *do* you do it?" said Bets. "You sent poor Mr. Goon out at sixty miles an hour! I bet he's puzzled – he didn't wait for 'I want Auntie!' "

"Serves him right," said Fatty. "What does he want to go and write an idiotic report about pigs and dogs and groaning men for? They weren't important. I bet he spread himself too – put in bits about snarling, and the patter of pigs' feet, and the sound of a wounded man dragging himself over the floor! I know Goon!"

"And now, I suppose, as he's told the Chief you were there, you'll be asked all about it too," said Bets. "Whatever will you say to him? Will you tell him it was all you?"

"I don't know," said Fatty, looking gloomy. "Blow
118

Goon! I bet he was worried in case I said I wouldn't back up his poppy-cock story. But I'll have to."

"Any more macaroons, Fatty?" asked Pip. "There's one left."

"No, thanks. This has rather spoilt my appetite," said Fatty.

"Well, you've had four macaroons, if not five, so you can't have much appetite left to spoil," remarked Larry. "Finish up the macaroon, Pip?"

Surprisingly enough no one wanted it. "I'll go a splash and buy it for Buster," said Pip. "He's been so good and quiet."

Buster was surprised and thrilled. He gulped the macaroon down at once.

"I call it a waste of a macaroon to gulp it down without a single crunch," said Pip, looking at Buster. "You dogs haven't learnt the art of eating yet. Wasn't he good with Goon this morning, Fatty?"

"Yes. He must have known Goon was in need of comfort, and wanted some one to hold his hand and say 'There, there' to him," said Fatty, still cross. "Gone all soft-hearted, Buster? Gah!"

They got up and went off to find their bicycles. Fatty paid the bill. It was a very large one, considering it was only for hot chocolate and macaroons. Still, as Fatty said, school was looming horribly on the horizon and they might as well make hay and eat macaroons while they could!

They biked back to Fatty's, as there was still an hour before lunch. "But we MUST leave in good time today," said Pip. "I really believe Mother will send us to bed on bread and water if we're late again. You're lucky not to have a fierce mother, Fatty."

"Oh, ours isn't *fierce*, Pip," said Bets, protesting. "She's just keen on rules being kept. I wouldn't change our mother for anything."

"Nor would I, idiot," said her brother. "But you can't deny she was pretty fierce yesterday. The thing is, we MUST leave early."

"Let's go down to the shed again," said Larry. "I left

a book there. It's a detective story I thought you mightn't have read, Fatty."

"Pooh! Fatty's read every single detective story that's ever been written!" said Bets. "He's ...why, Fatty, what's up?"

Fatty had thrown his bicycle suddenly to the ground when they came to the shed, and had rushed up to the door with a cry. He swung round.

"Some one's been here! The lock's forced! The door's ajar – and just LOOK at the inside of the shed!"

The five stared at the shed. Fatty had swung the door open – and inside were piled all the shed's contents in an incredible muddle. All Fatty's "disguises" had been torn from their pegs or from their chest and had been flung down. Boxes had been opened and their contents thrown out. It was a scene of utmost confusion and chaos.

"Oh, Fatty!" said Bets, trembling. "Oh, Fatty!"

"Look at that!" said Fatty, angrily. "That burglar fellow has been HERE – while we were out – and he's messed up everything – and what's more, I'll bet he's taken those dolls' clothes!"

Fatty was right. The precious clothes were gone. Their biggest, finest Clue! The box into which Fatty had thrown them was empty. Not even a sock was left! The thief had found at last what he had looked for so persistently.

Fatty sat down on a box and groaned. This was a real shock to him. "Why did we leave the things here?" he almost wailed. "Why didn't we take them with us? Now we're finished – nothing to show for all our work at all!"

"It must have been the thief we heard in the garden when we thought it was just your mother," said Larry. "Oh, Fatty – isn't this a blow?"

"Well, we can't take the clothes and tackle Mr. Fellows now," said Pip. "I don't see that there's anything we can do. Whatever made us leave the things here for the thief to get? And we even go out and leave the coast clear for him. We must have been mad."

120

"We were worse. We were fatheads," said Fatty, in deep dejection. "I blame myself. How could I be such a mutt?"

It was no good talking about it. The thing was done. The thief had come and gone and had taken what he wanted away with him. Fatty heard a sound near the shed and went out to see if it was the gardener.

It was. "Hedges, have you seen any stranger about this morning?" he asked. "Some one's been into my shed."

"Well, I'll be blowed!" said Hedges. "That would be that fellow with the scarred cheek, I expect. A nasty chap he looked. I turned him away once. He was trying to make me give him an order for manure. I found him in the garden! He said he was looking for me, Master Frederick – but I guess he was looking about for what he could steal."

Fatty nodded and went back to the others. He was very down in the dumps. "It was the water-weed man all right," he said. "The gardener said he had a scarred cheek, so that proves it was the fellow we know. Blow, blow, blow! I'll never forgive myself for this."

"Let's tidy up," said Bets. "We can't leave you to put everything back in its place by yourself. Come on, Daisy – I'll hand you Fatty's disguises to hang up."

Every one was soon busy putting the shed tidy again. It took quite a long time. As Bets was picking up a few things she gave a sudden exclamation.

"Look – the tiny hanky with daisies on it and the name Eurycles," she said. "The thief must have overlooked it or dropped it when he took all the other clothes."

Every one stared at it. "Well," said Fatty, fingering it, "you'd better keep it for yourself, Bets – it's not much good to us now."

Bets put the tiny hanky into her pocket. She felt rather bad. It was all that was left of their wonderful collection of clues. She went on tidying up everything with the others.

"Better shove all the rest of the things into that chest,"

said Fatty at last, looking at his watch. "You ought to go. It's getting near dinner-time."

So the last few armfuls were flung higgledy-piggledy into the chest, and the lid was shut down. Then the four got their bicycles, shouted good-bye to Fatty, and raced off.

Fatty went slowly back to the house. He was very depressed. Things had been going so well. Now all they had left of their biggest clue was the tiny hanky with Eurycles embroidered on it. And a fat lot of good that was, Fatty reflected. Was there much point in trying to find out if there was a ventriloquist called Mr. Eurycles? Fatty thought not. He was beginning to feel fed-up with the whole thing.

"Oh, there you are, Frederick," said his mother, as he came slowly in. "Dear me – you do look miserable! Cheer up! A great friend of yours telephoned this morning – but you were out, so he's telephoning this afternoon."

"Who's that?" asked Fatty, not at all interested. It was probably one of his school friends, he thought. How boring! He would see enough of them in a few days! Poor Fatty was indeed feeling depressed!

"It was Chief Inspector Jenks," said his mother, expecting Fatty to be delighted. He thought the world of the Chief, who knew all the children very well, and had often welcomed their help in many curious mysteries.

But, far from pleasing him, the news made Fatty feel more down in the dumps than ever. Now he'd have a very difficult and awkward telephone conversation with the Chief. Chief Inspector Jenks had a high opinion of Fatty's capabilities, but a low opinion of some of his jokes. Fatty felt that things were getting worse than ever.

He ate a very poor lunch, though whether it was because he was worried, or had had too many macaroons, he didn't know. Probably both, he thought.

The telephone rang immediately after the meal was ended. "That's the Chief Inspector, Frederick," said his mother. "You answer it, will you?"

Fatty went. He took down the receiver, "Hallo!" he said. "This is . . ."

"Ah, Frederick!" interrupted a voice. "It's you. Good. I wanted to speak to you."

"Delighted, sir," said Fatty, most untruthfully.

"Listen – I've had a most extraordinary report in from Goon," said the Chief. "He's sent in plenty of peculiar reports in his time – but this beats them all. It's so extraordinary that I didn't believe it. But when I telephoned him he not only swore it was true but said that you would back him up. He said you were a witness to all the things in his report – though why he didn't mention you were there, when he wrote his report, I don't know."

"Quite, sir," said Fatty, politely.

"Apparently Goon went to inspect a house that was empty and that had been reported as burgled," said the Chief, sounding very businesslike and brisk. "He says that there was a kitten there, mewing – a dog which growled most ferociously, and snarled, and was ready, so he infers, to eat him up – and a pig – a *pig*, P-I-G – that grunted somewhere and stamped about overhead – really, Frederick, I am ashamed to quote from this report!"

Fatty couldn't help grinning into the telephone. Goon had certainly let himself go!

"Go on, sir," he said.

"And to crown everything, Goon reports that there was a wounded man in the house, who was groaning and dragging himself about somewhere, crying out 'I never did it, I never. Oooooh, I never did it. Where's my Auntie?" It sounds quite incredible, Frederick."

"It does, sir," said Fatty, trying to keep his end of the phone very business-like, and not give away anything.

There was a pause. "Are you still there, Frederick?" said the Chief. "Well, I may as well tell you that as soon as Goon told me you were in the house with him, I smelt a rat! Not a dog or a pig or any other animal, Frederick, but a rat. Do you understand me?"

"Er – yes, I think I do, sir," said Fatty.

There was another pause. Then the Chief's voice came again, a harder note in it. "I imagine I am correct in thinking that you had something to do with the extraordinary things in this report?" he rapped out.

"Well, yes, sir," said Fatty, wishing this one-sided conversation would end. He didn't like the sound of the Chief's stern voice at all!

"Exactly what did you have to do with it?" asked the Chief. "Please be a little more explicit, Frederick. I'm getting tired of this yes-sir, no-sir business. You usually have plenty to say for yourself."

"Yes, sir. Well, it's like this," said Fatty, desperately. "I've been practising ventriloquism, and . . .'

"Practising *what*!"

"VENTRILOQUISM," shouted Fatty.

"Oh, ventriloquism," repeated the Chief. "Good heavens! I didn't think of that. Bless us all – *ventriloquism*! What next? What an absolute menace you are, Frederick. There's no other word for it – a Menace."

"Yes, sir," said Fatty, sensing that the Chief was not feeling *quite* so angry. "I say, sir – there's a bit of a mystery on here – and I want to get hold of a ventriloquist myself. A man called Mr. Eurycles. How can I find out about him?"

There was a startled pause. "Did you say Eurycles?" came the Chief's voice in amazement. "Now why do you want to see *him*? Wait – don't say a word more over the telephone – not a word. I'm coming straight over. Keep your mouth shut till I come!"

An Exciting Meeting

There was a click as the Chief put down his receiver. Fatty put back his too, feeling rather dazed. What an abrupt ending! Why was the Chief so astonished? Did he know about their little "Mystery" then? Did he actually know anything about Mr. Eurycles?"

It was all very puzzling. Fatty rubbed his nose. He wasn't altogether pleased at the idea of seeing Chief Inspector Jenks that afternoon. He didn't particularly want the subject of dogs and pigs and groaning men re-opened, and it might quite well be.

Mrs. Trotteville was curious to know what the conversation had been about. She had heard the word Ventriloquism, because Fatty had shouted it so loudly.

"What's this about ventriloquism, Frederick?" she asked. "Did I hear you say you were practising it? I do wish you wouldn't. I suppose that explains all those queer noises that keep coming from your room when you are up there alone."

"Yes, Mother. But don't you get all hot and bothered about it," said Fatty. "I'll be back at school in a very short time. Then the house will be nice and quiet. By the way – er – the Chief Inspector is coming over here this afternoon. Do you mind if I get the other four along? They'll like to see him – especially Bets."

"Yes – get them along if you like," said his mother. "But, Frederick – I hope all this doesn't mean you've been mixing yourselves up again in matters that don't concern you. I really did hope you'd not lead the others into trouble these holidays."

Fatty was indignant. "I *never* lead them into trouble! Mother, how can you say such a thing! Why, even the Inspector has often told me that . . ."

"All right, Frederick," said his mother. "I am not going to argue with you. Telephone the others and see if they can come to tea. There is a nice new batch of cakes in today – and I brought in some macaroons from the dairy. You haven't had any for a long time."

"Not so very long!" thought Fatty, pleased at the idea of a few more that afternoon. He went to telephone the others, but, remembering the Chief's injunction to "keep his mouth shut," he gave them no hint as to the unexpected visit, though he would dearly have liked Bets to know. She was very fond of the "high-up policeman", as she used to call him.

"It's a pity we've got to tell the Chief that we were

125

idiotic enough to leave the dolls' clothes unguarded, so that they were stolen," thought Fatty. "That won't be a very good mark for me! I can't think how I was such a fathead. Well, the deed is done."

The Chief arrived first, in his big, black, shiny car, driven by a police-driver, and, surprisingly, with him came a distinguished-looking man in plain clothes.

Fatty was at the door when the car came up the drive and stopped outside. He welcomed the Chief with pleasure. The big, burly, good-looking man grinned at Fatty.

"Well, you Menace? I've a good mind to cast you off and have no more to do with you!" He turned to the tall, quiet man by his side.

"Sir, this is the boy I was telling you about. He plagues the local police, but at times he's been very useful to me. He's dependable and responsible, so you can tell him what you like. Let me introduce Frederick Trotteville."

Fatty shook hands solemnly. He noticed that the Chief didn't tell him the tall man's name. It was obvious that he was a very Big Noise, Fatty thought. Probably in the Secret Service – or – Scotland Yard. Anyway, a bit hush-hush. Fatty looked at him in awe.

They all went into the sitting-room, where a bright fire was burning. Mrs. Trotteville had gone out to one of her bridge afternoons. Fatty was thankful. He didn't particularly want his mother to be present if his escapades with Goon were to be gone into.

They sat down. "Now, first of all, Frederick, what do you know about Mr. Eurycles?" asked the Chief, coming straight to the point as usual.

"Not much," confessed Fatty. "I'd better tell you everything from the beginning, sir, then you'll see how we finally arrived at Mr. Eurycles. It's a queer little story – we got mixed up in it somehow but it's rather interesting."

"Fire away," said the Chief, "we're listening. I may take a few notes as you relate your tale, but don't let that worry you. Now then?"

Fatty was just beginning his tale when he heard the

loud ringing of four bicycle bells, and Buster began to bark and paw at the door.

"Oh – it's the others, sir," said Fatty, apologetically. "Do you mind if they come in too? I mean – they were all in it."

"Fetch them in," said the Chief, and Fatty went to the window, threw it up, and yelled:

"I say, all of you! Come in here. Quick!"

The four parked their bicycles in a hurry, and rushed in at the garden door. What was up? They burst into the sitting-room, and stopped in amazement when they saw their old friend, Chief Inspector Jenks, tall and burly as ever, a wide smile on his good-humoured face.

Bets flung herself on him, and as usual he swung her high in the air and she shrieked. The others crowded round eagerly. What fun to see the Chief again – and how exciting! What did it mean?

The tall, quiet man also stood up, smiling. He seemed very much amused with all this. The Chief introduced the four new-comers to him, one by one. But again he did not say who the stranger was. The tall man was very courteous, and his shrewd, dark eyes rested in turn on each child's face. Fatty guessed that he didn't miss much!

"What have you come for? Not just to see *us*?" cried Bets.

"I came because I think you may have a tale to tell me that will help me in something else," said the Chief. "Frederick was just about to tell it when you arrived. Sit down, and we'll hear it."

Every one sat down, Bets as near the big Chief as she could possible get. Fatty began again.

He described the breaking into Mr. Fellows' house, and what the milkman had reported. He told how he and the others had gone to have a look at the house, which was so near Larry's.

"And, I suppose, you managed to find an excuse for a little breaking-in yourself, Frederick?" said the Chief.

"Well – there was a kitten left behind," said Fatty,

grinning. "And while I was looking for it in the house, Mr. Goon appeared."

"I see – and then the dog, and the pig, and the groaning man began to haunt the house too, I suppose," said the Chief. "All right, we won't go into details. I've had too many already from Goon. I know all this bit, actually. It was fully reported to me at once. Tell me the bits I'm not likely to know."

So Fatty told him of the question he had put to himself – who could have seen Fellows rushing out at night? He went on to describe his talks with the night-watchmen – and regretfully he decided that he must also tell of his impersonation of the old man with the sack, and describe how he had led Goon to the jetty and tipped in the sack of stones.

"Most reprehensible," murmured the Chief.

"Yes, sir," agreed Fatty, hurrying on. He told how the five of them had gone down to see if Goon would drag out the sack next day and what he would do when he found he had been spoofed – he described the watching water-weed man, which caused both the Chief and his plain-clothes friend to sit up straight and look at one another.

"Give me a full description of this man, please," said the Chief, and, helped by the others, Fatty gave a very full description indeed.

"Excellent," said the Chief. "Most observant lot you are! I wouldn't be surprised if you told me everything the fellow had in his pockets! Wait a minute now – you say Goon arrived just then?"

"Yes, sir," said Fatty. The Chief took a sheaf of papers from his pockets and chose one, which he read quickly to himself.

"This is Goon's report of that morning," he said. "But it's confused and lacks detail. I think we'd better get him along here too, now that he comes well into the tale. I may want to ask him a few questions."

"Shall I telephone him, sir?" said Larry, at once. What a wonderful meeting! Goon would just about complete it. Poor Goon – he didn't shine on these occasions.

The Chief nodded and began to make some notes, which he passed to the stranger. Larry telephoned, got Goon at once, and gave him the Chief's message.

"What did he say?" inquired the Chief, when Larry returned.

"Well – er – not much, sir," said Larry, embarrassed. "Actually he just said 'Lovaduck.' Nothing else."

Every one laughed. Bets began to play with Buster, but it wasn't more than two minutes before Goon came sailing up the drive on his bicycle. He was met at the door by Fatty, who ushered him solemnly into the rather crowded sitting-room.

Goon was very nervous. He hadn't taken off his bicycle clips, nor had he stopped to brush his uniform which showed traces of his dinner. He slipped his helmet off and put it on the floor.

"Sit down, Goon," said the Chief. "I'm glad you came so quickly. Er – we have been hearing quite an interesting little tale from Master Frederick, here, and we thought you should hear it too – though no doubt you already know a good deal."

Goon looked hurriedly and beseechingly at Fatty. He sat down heavily, and Buster at once capered round his ankles. Fatty called him off sternly.

"Shut up, Buster. This is a serious meeting." He turned to the Chief again. "Shall I go on, sir? Well, that morning, Mr. Goon did come down to the river, as we expected. And he took a boat and rowed to the jetty where I'd thrown in the sack of stones the night before."

A snort came from Goon, but nobody took any notice of it. "Mr. Goon found a sack, sir – but it wasn't the sack I'd thrown in – it was another one."

Goon stared at Fatty, his mouth open. What! That boy *hadn't* put in that sack? Then who had?

"Mr. Goon opened the sack, sir, and it was full of very peculiar things. Clothes, sir – dolls' clothes – coat, trousers, belt, tie, socks – and a glove to match the one I told you I'd found in Mr. Fellows' house. That made us guess the sack was the one that Fellows himself had hidden in the river – so we took all the clothes home."

"But wait a minute – how did you get them? I thought *Goon* had them in the sack he pulled up," said the Chief, puzzled.

"Well," said Fatty, looking embarrassed, "he – er – well, he *gave* them to me, sir. Gave me every single one! You look surprised – well, so was I!"

A Strange Tale

"But I don't understand," said the Chief. "These clothes were a most important clue. Goon, what in the world made you hand them over to Master Frederick?"

Mr. Goon swallowed hard. His face was going a peculiar colour. That boy! That Toad of a Boy! Here he was in trouble again because of That Boy. He couldn't think for the life of him what to answer.

But Bets answered for him. "He didn't *give* them to him," she said, indignantly. "He fell on Fatty and stuffed everything down his neck – all wet and slimy too!"

"Be quiet, Bets," said Fatty, uncomfortably. "I'd asked for it."

"What peculiar behaviour, Goon," said the Chief, astounded. "No wonder your report was hard to follow. Is it a habit of yours to stuff things down people's necks when you are annoyed?"

"No, sir," muttered Goon, his eyes on the floor. "How was I to know those clothes were important, sir? I wouldn't have stuffed them down his neck if I'd thought they'd got anything to do with this case. I was – well, I was downright annoyed that morning, sir."

"I didn't mind the fight," said Fatty earnestly, sorry for poor Goon at that moment. "As a matter of fact, I rather enjoyed it. It was jolly clever of Goon to stuff every single thing down my neck – shoes and all!"

"Shoes? Did you say *shoes*?" said the Chief, at once.

He made a quick note. "Well, we will now leave this subject of stuffing clothes down necks, as I see it is rather painful to Goon, and get on with the next part of the tale."

Fatty told how they had dried out the clothes - how there had been a breaking into his own house that night, but nothing was taken - how he had interviewed Mr. Fellows, and got nothing but evasions - and finally how they had examined the clothes that very morning and how Bets had made her interesting discovery.

Goon was now listening intently. This was all new to him.

"We found nothing of interest at all, sir," said Fatty "Until Bets here found a tiny pocket hidden in the sleeve-cuff - and in it was a handkerchief embroidered with daisies, and the name I told you - Eurycles. Bets, where's the hanky?"

Bets produced it proudly. In an intent silence the Chief and his friend examined it. Mr. Goon gaped. What was all this? What did a doll's handkerchief matter?

"What did you deduce from this handkerchief then?" asked the Chief.

"Well, first I recognized the name Eurycles," said Fatty.

The stranger spoke directly to Fatty for the first time.

"Why did you recognize it? It is not a usual name," he said.

"No, I know that, sir," said Fatty. "In fact I'd never met any one of that name in my life, though for all I know there may be plenty of Greeks called Eurycles. I recognized it because - well, because I'm a bit of a ventriloquist, as I told the Chief here. You see, there was once a Greek called Eurycles who was a very famous ventriloquist indeed. I read about him in my book on ventriloquism."

"Remarkable," said the stranger, in his soft voice. "And so you thought that the clothes must belong to a doll owned by a modern ventriloquist called Mr. Eurycles?"

"Yes, that's right," said Fatty. "I was at a dead end

131

as regards this mystery, and I thought perhaps if I could find out if there *really* was a ventriloquist using the old Greek name as a stage name, I could ask him a few questions. I thought *he* might be able to solve this peculiar mystery for us. That's why I asked the Chief on the telephone if he knew of any one called Eurycles and how I could get in touch with him."

"I see. Again I say – it's most remarkable," said the tall man. "Well – you'll be interested to know that there is a modern ventriloquist who uses Eurycles as his stage name – and that those clothes you speak of, do belong to his doll. And you'll also be interested to know that we have been searching everywhere for the clothes."

"Why?" asked Fatty, astonished. "Gosh, what a lot of people are interested in those clothes!"

"I propose to tell you a little story myself now," said the Chief's friend. "A story which you must keep to yourselves. You are not to ask me any questions about it, you must accept my tale as it stands. It will tell you why my friend, the Chief Inspector here, was amazed when you spoke of Mr. Eurycles to him."

This was all very astonishing. Every eye was on the quiet stranger as he began his tale.

"You know the Chief Inspector and you know that I am a friend of his, in the same kind of service – we work to preserve the law and order of our country, to keep out enemies, to secure for this country the things that are right and proper."

He paused. Every one felt very solemn, and Bets found that she was holding her breath.

"Very well. It is our duty to discover and watch any man or woman who is working against this country and its laws. There are many of them, some in high-up places, some in lowly ones. Our duty is to watch, to sift out what we hear, and to report whenever we find any one suspected of misdeeds against the country and its laws."

"Spies?" whispered Bets.

"Not only spies – but any man or woman of evil intent," said the tall man. "Mr. Eurycles was one who
132

helped us in this. He was a clever ventriloquist who went everywhere with Bobby-Boy, his Talking Doll. He went to both high and low places, and gathered a great deal of information for us. Mr. Fellows was his assistant."

"Oh!" cried Daisy. "Was he really? So that's how *he* comes in!"

"One day one of Mr. Eurycles' friends came to him with a list of names," went on the Chief's friend. "They were names that we wanted more than anything else! Names of people undermining every industry in our country – provoking strikes, sabotage, anything that would harm Britain – and there was also other information, very valuable indeed to us. Mr. Eurycles put the information into his usual hiding-place – in the clothes that Bobby-Boy wore."

Everyone listened intently, especially Mr. Goon.

"That night Mr. Eurycles was kidnapped. The kidnappers took Bobby-Boy also, knowing that either on Mr. Eurycles or on his doll the list of names was hidden. But the ventriloquist managed to throw the doll out of the window of the car that kidnapped him.

"Following the car was one of our police-cars, as it happened – not because the police suspected that Mr. Eurycles was in the first car, but because they knew it to be a stolen car. When the doll was thrown out, the police in the car behind thought it was a small child and stopped their car, of course, to see.

"They lost the first car and returned to headquarters. Mr. Fellows had by then reported the kidnapping of his master, the ventriloquist, so the doll, Bobby-Boy, was handed to him. Apparently he knew that Mr. Eurycles had hidden something of value in the clothes, but he had no idea what. So he took the clothes into his keeping, hoping that his master would soon turn up."

"Oh, *I* see! And then the kidnappers found out that the list wasn't on Mr. Eurycles but somewhere in the doll's clothes, and have been hunting for it ever since!" cried Daisy.

"And that's why Fellows ran out with the clothes in
133

the middle of the night, when some one broke into his house – and he sank them into the river, meaning to get them again sometime," said Pip, seeing everything now. "And then the water-weed man, who was the burglar, saw Mr. Goon stuffing them down Fatty's neck, and so the next place he broke into was Fatty's. Goodness, we were in the middle of something terribly exciting, and we didn't know it!"

"Why didn't Mr. Fellows look for the valuable list himself and take it?" asked Bets. "Then he could have thrown the clothes away."

"I imagine that he wasn't able to find it – and anyway he didn't know what to look for," said the Chief. "But *we* shall be able to find it. We have had information as to where it is. If you'll just produce the clothes, Frederick, we will show you where the invaluable list is hidden, a most dramatic ending to what you called 'just a little Mystery'!"

There was a dead silence. All the excitement drained out of the children as they remembered the disastrous happening of the morning.

"What's the matter?" said the Chief, surprised. "You *have* got the clothes here, haven't you? What are you looking like that for?"

"It's awful to have to tell you, sir – but they're gone," said Fatty, in a low voice. "We – we went out of the shed where we kept them, locked it behind us, and when we got back the shed was broken open – and all the clothes were gone."

Bets burst into tears. "What shall we do? Oh, we didn't know it was so important! Oh, Fatty, what shall we do?"

The Chief Inspector whistled through his teeth and looked at his plain-clothes friend.

"This is a set-back!" he said. "A real shock. Our scarred-faced friend again, I suppose. He's certainly determined this time!"

"That list is important to him – and to a lot of others who would like it destroyed," said the tall man, grimly. "And, unfortunately, it is important to us too." He turned to Fatty.

"*All* the clothes went – he took the lot?" he asked sharply.

"Yes – all except for the little hanky Bets found, which you've seen," said Fatty. "But if you like we can go down to my shed and have another look in the box where we put them. But I'm pretty certain it's empty, sir."

They trailed down to the shed, Mr. Goon too, all of them feeling most depressed. To have such an exciting mystery – and then to have the right ending snatched away just as they were being so successful! It really was bad luck.

They looked into the box. It was, as Fatty said, well and truly empty. Then Bets suddenly remembered something and cried out loudly.

"The shoe that Buster took! Did we find it and hide that away too? Or did we forget it and leave it in whatever corner Buster put it?"

"We forgot it. I didn't put it in," said Fatty. "But would just one shoe be of any use to you, sir?"

"My word, yes – more than you'd think, if it was the right shoe!" said the Chief. "Here, Buster boy, find that shoe!"

And, as if Buster completely understood, he ran round the shed, hunting into this corner and that – and finally, after sniffing under an old sack, he disappeared beneath it, worried at something – and came out proudly with a doll's red shoe in his mouth!

"It's the shoe. He's found it," said Fatty, in delight. "Good old Buster. Clever dog, Buster."

Buster wagged his tail proudly. The Chief took the shoe at once and he and his friend examined it closely.

"It may be the one. Can't tell without examining it," said the Chief. "Any one got a sharp pen-knife?"

Fatty had, of course. He always kept his pockets full of things that might conceivably come in useful some day.

The Chief took the knife and sat down on a box. He turned the shoe upside down, and, with all the Find-Outers breathing heavily down his neck, he began to try and prize away the heel.

"Strongly made," said the Chief. "Ah – up it comes!"

The heel came away from the shoe, and the children saw a neat little hollowed-out compartment in the heel itself. In it was a thin sheet of paper tightly folded.

"It's here," cried the Chief, as excited as the five children. His fingers delicately eased the paper from its hiding-place. He handed it, folded, to the tall man, whose eyes were now gleaming.

He unfolded the paper very carefully, and ran his eyes down a list of names and notes. They were all written in most minute writing, impossible to make out at a distance. Mr. Goon, craning his neck to see if he could read anything, could only make out a blur.

"This is it," said the tall man, a ring of triumph in his voice. "There's a whole year's work here – invaluable, Jenks! And to think how nearly we lost it – if it hadn't been for that dog running off with the shoe as he did, and hiding it, we'd have lost it for good!"

"The thief must just have seen the bundle of clothes in the box, thought everything was there, and picked the whole lot up," said Fatty. "And gone off with it in delight. What a shock when he finds only one shoe!"

136

"Perhaps he'll come back and try and find it," suggested Larry. "You could catch him then."

"Oh, we know where to pick him up now," said the Chief. "My word – look at this name on the list – and that – whew! This is going to make a stir!"

"It is. It's going to make several dozen people extremely uncomfortable," said the tall man, grimly. "What a haul! I can't believe it – and all because of these kids. Marvellous, aren't they!"

"Well – they've certainly done some good work in their time," said the Chief, smiling. "Very good work. They call themselves the Five Find-Outers and Dog, you know. And the things they've found out – they could really have books and books written about them!"

"But Buster's really the hero of *this* Mystery!" said Bets, picking up the little Scottie and hugging him. "Aren't you, Buster? Did you know that shoe was important, Buster? Is that why you hid it? Fatty, I'd be quite ready to believe that Buster *did* guess, you know!"

"What are you going to do now?" asked Larry, turning to the Chief.

"Well, just a few bits of work," said the Chief. "We must go and drop in on Fellows, to begin with, and set his mind at rest. And we must send somebody to gather in Mr. Scarred-Face – or the water-weed man, as you call him. He won't be wanting water-weed for some time after this!"

"I do so hope you'll get Mr. Eurycles back some day," said Bets. "I hope nothing horrid's happened to him."

"I'll let you know when he does appear again," said the Chief. "I have a feeling that once we get after the people whose names are on this sheet of paper, our Mr. Eurycles will find himself unexpectedly free. Quite a lot of these people will flee the country soon!"

"Er – can't we give these children a little reward for their enormous help?" said the tall man, getting up from his box and almost bumping his head against the roof.

137

"Oh, no thank you," said Fatty at once. "That would spoil everything – we wouldn't want to solve mysteries for a reward. We do it because it's fun – and we like helping the Chief."

"My dear fellow, there are so few people left in the world who will do things without expecting payment or reward, that I think we'll let the Find-Outers go their own good way," said the Chief to his friend, quite seriously. That made the five feel extremely proud.

"Right," said the tall man. "Well, we must be going. Still, there are two things I'm going to do for these er – what do they call themselves – these Find-Outers and Dog. I am going to get my butcher to send his biggest and juiciest bone to this remarkably clever dog. . . ."

"Wuff," said Buster, wagging his tail most appreciatively.

"And when Mr. Eurcyles turns up again I shall ask him if he would be good enough to give Frederick here a few first-class lessons in ventriloquism," said the tall man. "He'll be delighted to do that."

Fatty blushed with pleasure. "Oh, sir – thank you. I don't want any reward, as you know – and I'll pay for the lessons. Gosh, wouldn't I like them! Thanks awfully."

The Chief and his friend departed. The police car revved up and disappeared down the drive. Only Mr. Goon was left with the five children. They looked at one another.

Poor old Goon. He hadn't had much of a look in this time. The Chief hadn't even said a word of farewell to him. Even Buster had done better than Goon!

"Well," said Fatty in a jovial tone, "what about tea? It must surely be ready by now. Anyway, *I'm* ready for it. Mr. Goon – will you join us?"

Mr. Goon was so astounded at this invitation that he could only gape. He was not a generous enemy, like Fatty, and never would be. He hardly understood this invitation, and his mouth opened and shut like a gold-fish.

"Well, do answer, Mr. Goon," said Fatty. "We'll cele-brate the occasion, and I'll open the big tin of chocolate biscuits I got for Christmas. Will you, won't you, will you, won't you, Mr. Goon?"

"I will," gasped Goon, almost as if he was getting married. "Thanks. I take it very kind of you after – er – after some of the things that have happened."

"Well, don't you go stuffing things down my neck again!" said Fatty, leading the way in.

"Goon gave a sudden grin. "And don't you go making up dogs, and pigs, and what-not," he said.

Bets didn't want Goon to stay to tea, but she said nothing. She liked Fatty's generous gesture, and she knew that poor Mr. Goon hadn't had a very good time in this mystery – but nothing was going to persuade her to sit next to him, or even to address a word to him. She would never, never forgive him for stuffing those things down Fatty's neck, and almost squashing him to death!

It was a most hilarious tea. Every one was pleased that the little Mystery had turned out to be a Genuine, Large-Size one, and had ended so triumphantly for Bus-ter.

Buster, of course, was amazed to find his old enemy suddenly belonging to the family circle. He gave a few fierce growls, and then as every one made so much fuss of him, and Daisy actually addressed him as Hero Dog, he joined in the general enjoyment.

Mr. Goon enjoyed himself too. Well, well – to think that Toad of a Boy could behave like this! After his fourth macaroon, and third piece of chocolate cake, Mr. Goon was ready to be Fatty's best friend.

And then a loud grunting noise was heard under the table! "What's that," cried Bets, in alarm. Mr. Goon looked under the table, amazed. Only Buster was there.

The others looked at Fatty's grinning face and
139

laughed. And then, from just behind the astounded Mr. Goon came an all-too-familiar voice:

"I never did it. I never! Ooooh, I never did! Where's my Auntie?"

Oh, Fatty! What are we to do with you? Tell us about your next Mystery, do!

ENID BLYTON is Dragon's bestselling author. Her books have sold millions of copies throughout the world and have delighted children of many nations. Here is a list of her books available in Dragon Books:

FIRST TERM AT MALORY TOWERS	35p ☐
SECOND FORM AT MALORY TOWERS	35p ☐
THIRD YEAR AT MALORY TOWERS	35p ☐
UPPER FOURTH AT MALORY TOWERS	35p ☐
IN THE FIFTH AT MALORY TOWERS	30p ☐
LAST TERM AT MALORY TOWERS	35p ☐
MALORY TOWERS GIFT SET	£2.25 ☐
6 Books ENID BLYTON	

THE TWINS AT ST. CLARE'S	35p ☐
SUMMER TERM AT ST. CLARE'S	35p ☐
SECOND FORM AT ST. CLARE'S	35p ☐
CLAUDINE AT ST. CLARE'S	35p ☐
FIFTH FORMERS AT ST. CLARE'S	35p ☐
THE O'SULLIVAN TWINS	35p ☐
ST. CLARE'S GIFT SET	£2.25 ☐
5 Books ENID BLYTON	

MYSTERY OF THE BANSHEE TOWERS	35p ☐
MYSTERY OF THE BURNT COTTAGE	30p ☐
MYSTERY OF THE DISAPPEARING CAT	30p ☐
MYSTERY OF THE HIDDEN HOUSE	30p ☐
MYSTERY OF HOLLY LANE	35p ☐
MYSTERY OF THE INVISIBLE THIEF	30p ☐
MYSTERY OF THE MISSING MAN	30p ☐
MYSTERY OF THE MISSING NECKLACE	30p ☐
MYSTERY OF THE PANTOMIME CAT	30p ☐
MYSTERY OF THE SECRET ROOM	30p ☐
MYSTERY OF THE SPITEFUL LETTERS	30p ☐
MYSTERY OF THE STRANGE BUNDLE	30p ☐
MYSTERY OF THE STRANGE MESSAGES	30p ☐
MYSTERY OF TALLY-HO COTTAGE	30p ☐
MYSTERY OF THE VANISHED PRINCE	30p ☐

CHILDREN'S LIFE OF CHRIST	30p ☐

THE BOY WHO TURNED INTO AN ENGINE	30p ☐
THE BOOK OF NAUGHTY CHILDREN	20p ☐
A SECOND BOOK OF NAUGHTY CHILDREN	35p ☐

PONY BOOKS are very popular with boys and girls.
Dragon Books have a fine selection by the best authors to choose from:

SPECIAL DELIVERY	Gillian Baxter	35p ☐
PANTOMIME PONIES	Gillian Baxter	35p ☐
SILVER BRUMBY'S KINGDOM	Elyne Mitchell	30p ☐
SILVER BRUMBIES OF THE SOUTH		
	Elyne Mitchell	30p ☐
SILVER BRUMBY	Elyne Mitchell	30p ☐
SILVER BRUMBY'S DAUGHTER	Elyne Mitchell	30p ☐
MY FRIEND FLICKA PART 1	Mary O'Hara	30p ☐
MY FRIEND FLICKA PART 2	Mary O'Hara	30p ☐
GREEN GRASS OF WYOMING 1	Mary O'Hara	25p ☐
GREEN GRASS OF WYOMING 2	Mary O'Hara	25p ☐
GREEN GRASS OF WYOMING 3	Mary O'Hara	25p ☐
THUNDERHEAD 1	Mary O'Hara	25p ☐
THUNDERHEAD 2	Mary O'Hara	25p ☐
THUNDERHEAD 3	Mary O'Hara	25p ☐
FOR WANT OF A SADDLE		
	Christine Pullein-Thompson	30p ☐
IMPOSSIBLE HORSE	Christine Pullein-Thompson	30p ☐
THE SECOND MOUNT	Christine Pullein-Thompson	25p ☐
THE EMPTY FIELD	Christine Pullein-Thompson	35p ☐
THREE TO RIDE	Christine Pullein-Thompson	35p ☐
THE PONY DOPERS	Christine Pullein-Thompson	35p ☐
A SWISS ADVENTURE	Pat Symthe	25p ☐
A SPANISH ADVENTURE	Pat Symthe	25p ☐

All these books are available at your local bookshop or newsagent, or can be ordered direct from the publisher. Just tick the titles you want and fill in the form below.

Name ....

Address ....

....

Write to Dragon Cash Sales, PO Box 11, Falmouth, Cornwall TR10 9EN. Please enclose remittance to the value of the cover price plus:
UK: 18p for the first book plus 8p per copy for each additional book ordered to a maximum charge of 66p. BFPO and EIRE: 18p for the first book plus 8p per copy for the next 6 books, thereafter 3p per book. OVERSEAS: 20p for the first book and 10p for each additional book.
Granada Publishing reserve the right to show new retail prices on covers, which may differ from those previously advertised in the text or elsewhere.